# Silence & Noise

## one girl's journey into insanity

a novel by
Casey Renee Le'Vasseur

Cover Photo and Author Photograph by Anthony Scarlati
Cover Design By Colin Montgomery

Copyright © 2009 Casey Renee Le'Vasseur
ISBN: 1463750072
ISBN-13: 978-1463750077
www.CRLWrites.com

For the lost and broken hearted.  The hurting and beaten down.

# A Note From The Author

This book is a work of fiction. While this story was inspired in part by moments I have experienced, have been told about, or witnessed, the characters in this story are not representations of real individuals. This is Lily's story, but maybe it's your story too.

# a voice in the darkness.

I have loved three times in my life. Two boys and one man. I have teetered on the edge. I have looked down. And I have fallen. Countless times I have imagined love. I have fabricated. I allowed myself to be consumed by something. So often I called it love, but it was not love.

On the surface this is a story about a girl who loves. A snapshot of social interaction, masking something bigger, something a little too complicated. The journey of a girl who feels an unequivocal desire to feel, constantly. A girl tormented by her emotions.

No, this is not a love story; this is far from a love story. This is an exploration of reason, this is a journey into the imagination. This is the back and forth caused by an inability to shut it off. This is the longing for something more and the impossibility of letting go. This is far from a fairytale, but this is one person's reality. The story of one girl's descent into madness.

# Prologue

## we don't say those things here.

I had a crazy aunt growing up. Some great aunt or something twice removed. There were the whispers. There were the *don't tell* moments. The *can she hear us? The feeling sorry for.* And those things, they weren't right.

*A tall much too thin woman is standing in the kitchen of a small home. Boxes, clutter, things, junk, all stacked up around her as far as the eye can see. She just stands there in the dimly lit room, the sunlight trying desperately to force itself through the small sliver of window unobstructed from the clutter. Out of the stark silence there is a knock at the door.*

*The woman, almost cautious makes her way down a small path to the front door. She peeks out to see a petite woman and two young girls standing at her doorstep. She turns to walk back to the kitchen, then hesitating, opens up the door just a crack.*

*"Hi Suzy, the girls and I brought you some dinner," the woman on the doorstep hands her a foil casserole dish.*

*The youngest of the two girls stares past Suzy, her eyes find their way through the small opening of the door and she takes it all in, holding tightly to her mother's leg. The older girl stands tall, unfazed.*

Casey Renee Le'Vasseur

*The woman snatches up the food and slams the door, no hello or thank you uttered.*

Those feelings. Insanity, it was destructive and it was impossible, and I was okay. In time everything would pass and I would gain some sanity back. But there was the *you're ok, don't worry, it's fine.* And there were my fits. There was me, as a child, my tantrums. The stubborn, set in my ways. The *everything is going wrong and I can't handle it* screaming matches. And there was the quiet. There was the, *not talking, not thinking, not feeling.* There were the tiny black clouds that turned a sweet girl into a demon. There were these impulsive acts that seemed normal. Felt typical. There were the late nights, over thinking. There were the stories spinning. All of these things present, even then. And I kept my silence. I don't know what it was, how it started. How I quieted my words, my emotions. How the stuffing began. Something inside of me begging to stay silent. Was it a memory, so faded now it has slipped away? Was it a thought, so dark it seemed out of reach? Whatever it was, it was there and it happened and it changed everything. Nowhere to go. No one to talk to. Everyone so busy with their own lives, me not wanting to be a bother. Not knowing what to say. How to word this. Knowing something wasn't right. Can't put your finger on it, figure it out. And it came from somewhere, started somewhere. And in time that thing, it grew. And it became a monster, and as I grew, he magnified. Everything magnified. And you hear people all the time commenting on other people's mental states. Assumptions. Finger pointing. But the truth is, it's impossible to understand. To put a finger on it. The complexity of it, of the emotions. And you try to fix it, try to drink it away, try to overcome it. You take your pills and try to wipe it out, try to make it fade away, like all those memories. But it's stagnant. There's no overcoming it, so you just have to survive with it. You just live with it. With the, *I guess this will be good enough.* You live with it. And it comes alive in you.

And me, my name is Lily. I'm 22 years old, and to be honest, I never thought I'd make it to this day. Not that 22 is some magical number, it's just a long way from 15. I never thought much beyond anything. And to my surprise, here I am. Not quite sure how I arrived at this moment, some great power at work, maybe. Whatever it was, I am here. And at this moment I really don't know much else, other than me being present on this earth.

There is not a lot I remember. There is so much that I have blacked out. So many moments lived and hidden away. So much truth replaced with lies. But maybe my truths are not reality, my feelings are not facts. I am not sure if there was a time when things were much different. The mind of a person like me, it's no mind at all, it can't be trusted. There were pieces of a life. Parts of me that have been squashed. Covered. Removed. On the journey, the road that brought me back to myself, back to the truth, it was long. Full of twists and bends. It was unending. It was my road, it is my road, and I am searching for the things I lost along the way. I am looking for an explanation, a reason for my existence. But more than anything, I am looking for a little truth, a memory not clouded by my misery. But the things you find, they always surprise you. Those things, you never expect them.

*Part 1*

# Chapter 1

## a beginning.

It was 1986 and there isn't much I remember, but I've heard stories. The thing with stories is they are only true for the person who is telling them. As the storyteller we take liberties with our words. We tell and re-tell, create and re-create so much that we forget the genuine memory. Our stories become new memories and to us, they are cold hard facts. We stubbornly cling to our memories as if they hold the answers to our existence. We are right, and everyone else is wrong. So it goes to say that my memories are fabricated by an overactive imagination. They are merely one person's interpretation of a lifetime of moments shared by others, but they are my memories, my moments. Some are fed by other people's memories of things I'm not sure if I truly remember experiencing or not. That's the fascinating part about these stories, you hear them so many times they become real to you. I hope one day I get the chance to watch my life on the big screen like a film so I can fact check myself. But, it is sort of nice remembering those big and not so big moments and believing they are all so true. I'd hate to be disappointed.

So, like I said, it was 1986. I'm sure a lot of great things happened that year. Some big wins in sports, some classic films released, some must have trends, some major moments. I imagine it was a pretty important time in history, but I don't remember any of that. All I remember is, incubating in my mother's womb, fighting for my freedom. Well, actually at some point there was me in my mother's womb fighting for my life, or death, whichever is easier for you to grasp. Thumb in mouth, fingers tightly clinging to the umbilical cord, cutting off my air supply. What was I thinking?

*Jenny, a petite pregnant woman, about to pop, lies on an examination table in a stark white room. Her curly brown hair forms ringlets around her face as her dark brown eyes stare up intently at the man in the white coat beside her. A male doctor stands by the table, staring at an ultrasound screen. There is a nurse at his side, everyone in their bright whites, blending in to the blank space. The doctor points at the screen.*

*"Is she okay?" Jenny asks as she turns her head toward the screen.*

*"It appears she is sucking on her thumb and gripping her hand on the umbilical cord. She is cutting off her oxygen," he says with concern.*

*"What are you gonna do, is she going to be okay?" Jenny cries.*

*The doctor places the ultrasound wand back on Jenny's stomach and continues to watch the screen. He taps gently on her stomach, while his eyes are fixated on the baby. He turns and looks at Jenny.*

*"I'll need you to turn on your stomach and prop yourself up on your knees," he explains.*

*"You want me to get on all fours?" Jenny questions with an air of confusion.*

*"Well, that's one way to put it," he jokes. "It will help take the pressure off the baby and hopefully loosen her grip so we can get her some oxygen."*

*Jenny turns over, clumsily holding up her 8 month's pregnant body. Trying to save her daughter's life.*

I try to picture it, as I was told. It's a little funny how much everyone cares when you are tiny and incapable of helping yourself, but when it all gets so real, people just start making excuses for themselves. And you, well, you start making excuses for yourself too.

My mom, was she worried, was she annoyed? Did this really happen, or is it just another memory someone made up? Either way it's a part of my history now, though it's hard to imagine that even then a monster was growing inside me.

When the time finally came for me to exit said womb, as the story goes, I flew out of there so fast I almost dropped to the floor. Take me back to that white room, to the beginning.

> *The doctor, dressed in pale blue scrubs and a white coat standing in front of Jenny's spread legs. The nurse in unison with him, handing him tools, and wiping his forehead with a damp cloth. Danny, the father planted at his wife's side as she squeezes his hands until the blood flows out. Jenny grits her teeth and as her face tightens, Danny winces in pain.*
>
> *"Give me one last push," the Doctor urges.*
>
> *Jenny growls something inaudible under her breath. Danny detaches her fingers from his hand.*
>
> *"I want to see her," he explains as he runs to the doctor's side.*
>
> *Just as Danny gets to the doctor a baby flies out from between Jenny's legs. The doctor put his hands out and the placenta covered baby slides through his fingers into Danny's arms. A bright eyed look of shock ignites his face as he stares down at his little girl. The doctor and nurse rush to his side, inspecting this little miracle child. The little baby sucking her mucus covered thumb.*

Me, so desperate for a change of scenery even then, before I could formulate the words. At this point maybe I should trace my desire to run, to escape back to that very moment. Sometimes I imagine Dad dropping me, and how easy it could have been, how many problems that would have solved.

And those two moments, they say more about me than anything else. They have defined my life or my life has been defined by them. That is the part I can't figure out. And they were just stories someone told me. And then they became my stories, and I told them, and everything makes perfect sense because of them. And it sort of makes me wonder if all that we are is made clear as we sit there, incubating in the womb. As our minds are formed, and we lie cushioned from the evils of the world, as we float forced to listen to or participate in whatever our mothers put us through. Is it then that we become who we really are? Or is that way too farfetched? It's probably some sort of combination of living mixed with waiting and it's all seasoned with the words we are told and the words we tell.

# Chapter 2

## a family of sorts.

The journey began before anyone realized. Married, young, too young maybe. A life of endless possibilities. Then the babies arrive and life as they know it, well, it just ends. I was born into a world with an older sister. A girl with her own demons, and she fills in a lot of gaps of memory. And me, I just shrug when the family gathers around and delves into our history.

*A small rental home, modestly decorated, is stuffed full of people; family and friends. The rickety dining table, surrounded by bodies, is covered in a clean tablecloth with slightly tattered edges. Platters of food are meticulously placed across the surface. The food line files through the kitchen, to the table, and flows into the living room where adults are plopped on various scattered chairs and couch corners. A group of kids play in the corner. A young girl with short brown hair, and deep dark eyes, sucks her thumb while simultaneously twirling a chunk of her hair in her fingers. She leans her body against a girl a couple years older, similar features. The older girl reads a book with one of the other kids. The thumb sucker, she just stares down the hallway, yanking her hair with each suck.*

*In the kitchen Jenny is scrambling to plate more food and Danny is leaning up against the counter watching her, smiling.*

*"Are you just gonna stand there, or are you helping?"* Jenny jabs.

*Danny smiles and wraps his arms around her waist. She tries to squirm out of his grasp and gives up. He kisses her, then releases his grip.*

*"Do you think everything looks alright? Are people having a good time?" she questions.*

*"It's fine, everything is fine," Danny takes a platter from the counter and walks into the dining room.*

*Jenny turns around and meets eyes with Lily, standing with a stuffed animal wrapped in her arms, thumb in mouth, hair in hand. Jenny laughs and walks to Lily, picking her up in her arms and carrying her back down the hall, into the living room. Bodies crammed in, stuffing their faces with food. A woman on the couch is rambling on.*

*"I like how you decorated Jenny," the woman compliments.*

*Jenny plops Lily on the ground beside her sister.*

*"Thanks, we still have a lot to do," Jenny starts.*

*"Well, it's a big leap from that little shack." The woman continues, "Didn't you guys have to bathe outside?"*

*An older woman with light red hair on the other side of the room jumps in.*

*"They had a tub, they just didn't have a shower. They were only there a few months," the redhead corrects.*

*"Well, there was no heat right?" the woman looks up at Jenny.*

*Jenny fiddles with some papers on a desk in the living room, all eyes on her. Danny enters the living room and walks to Jenny's side.*

*"I think the heat was out for a week or two. That place was fun," a slight smile appears on Danny's face.*

*He squeezes Jenny lightly and they look down at their little girls playing in the corner.*

I close my eyes, remembering the swing in the backyard of that old shack. We would just go back and forth and it was carefree, and there are pictures of me holding on for dear life. And it was real. And I wish I could remember the other stuff. But for a lot of years all there was is a swing. People make careers of tracing our personalities back to our histories, our upbringings, our memories, stories, lies, and truths. But what if none of that has anything to do with anything? Maybe it's all genetic, has nothing to do with environment.

Despite the good, the bad, the whatever, we were a family. And I think we were all relatively happy. At least the kids were, but I never had a reason to question anything. While everyone else is thinking "How can they pull this one off?" "They are drowning, barely standing." But the view is always different from the outside. And all I really remember is freedom.

As we got a little older, still young, but old enough to do the basics ourselves, my sister, Samantha, and I became latch-key kids. Mom and Dad, both busy building careers. Long days turned into business dinners. And the afternoons, the few hours between school ending and them getting home, that was our time. Those hours, days, years, all of that time accumulated, all of those memories formed, and they were ours to keep.

We would spend most afternoons daydreaming. Playing house. Drive-thru restaurants. Musicians. Artists. We were whatever we wanted to be. Doctors. Chefs. Criminals. Fishing in the sewers after a big rain. We were free. And everything was perfect. But when I think back, when I remember the details, when I sift through the rose colored frames and find the dust of the memories, it covers me, and everything makes sense again. And I wish it were more complicated. But I can see it all so clearly, no matter how much dirt I try to bury it in.

There is always something negative attached to a mental disorder. This stigma. This finger-pointing, whispering. They are crazy people on the street corners you just stare at. You judge them. The people shaking in the corner, talking to themselves. All these obvious examples of insanity. And this is a bad thing. This is something you run from. This is the *I am glad I am not that,* feeling sorry for, mocking. And the impossibilities they create inside of a person are endless. I remember all the talk about these people growing up, and trying to remind myself I was sane. Trying to remind myself that all these things I thought, felt. They were nothing. They weren't real. They were only passing clouds. Nothing permanent. There was no need for conversation. There was no need for exposure. I knew that my thoughts, my feelings, whatever I didn't understand at the time that was burning inside of me. Those things. We don't speak of those things.

## Chapter 3

## the days we forget.

The moods back then were irrational. But I was young and they were moods and that didn't mean a whole lot. My parents scratching their heads, trying to figure out where I came from. Why one minute I had a smile and the next my head was spinning. It was *not enough sleep*. It was *too tired to think*. It was *who knows*. Trying to make excuses.

I remember one afternoon doing a school project, I was maybe five or six. My mind trying to process the complexity of a squirrel. My eyes scanning thru the work sheet.

*Lily sits Indian style on a beige carpeted floor. Worksheets, folders, and school books are neatly placed around her. A thin veil of light flows in from outside, reflecting itself off the white walls. She holds a pencil as she stares down at a piece of paper in her hand. She tosses the paper on the ground and puts her head in her hands. Her little fingers form fists and she sits there for a moment, not moving.*

*There is the sound of a door closing at the other end of the house and Lily's eyes pop open. She grabs her paper and trips over herself running out of the bedroom. She finds her mother in the kitchen dressed in a skirt suit, heels and hose. Her mom is balancing groceries, and a purse, and mail, almost toppling over as she walks to the counter. Lily runs to her side, tugging gently on her purse.*

*"Mom, mom, I need help. I don't understand this project and I have to…," she starts, before her mother cuts her off midsentence.*

*"Lily, I just got home, give me a minute," Jenny urges as she plops everything down on the counter.*

*"But I need help now, I just don't know how…," Lily cries.*

*"Lily, stop whining, I will help you later, not now. If that isn't good enough you can ask your father. He should be home soon," Jenny demands.*

*Lily stomps her feet and leaves the kitchen, head down, blood simmering beneath the surface. She storms her way back into the bedroom and slams her worksheet down on the floor.*

*Lily opens a book and positions her body so that she is lying on her stomach. She picks up the yellow pencil and scribbles in the margin of the book. The force of her hand leaving dark graphite lines throughout. Her hands and body slightly twitching in unison.*

*Her father, Danny, enters the room. Home from work, he's changed into dirty jeans and a baseball cap, his brown hair peeking from the edges. He stands in the doorway, looking down at Lily. She doesn't look up.*

*"Honey, your mom said you needed some help?" he questions.*

*Lily halts her scribbling and slowly lies her pencil down on the book, letting it gently roll to the center. She reaches for the worksheet and scans the words.*

*"It says we have to do a project about an animal and describe its habitat or something, and I got a squirrel and we have to draw something and I don't know what to…," she rambles.*

*"Why don't you let me look at it?" Danny says as he sits down beside her.*

*Lily hands him the paper and he scans it.*

*"Well it looks like you just need to read about squirrels in the encyclopedia and do a description of everything," Danny explains.*

*"I know, that's not everything, there is a bunch of other stuff," Lily urges.*

*"Well, you just need to draw the squirrel in its environment," he adds.*

*Lily bends the corners of the book with her fingers. Her hands almost forming fists, and then releasing themselves, repeatedly.*

*"I don't know how to do all this stuff, it's too hard, I just need help," Lily begs.*

*Her father stands up and puts the worksheet back down.*

*"Lily, I think you can figure this out, it won't be hard," he assures her.*

*She slams her hands down on the book, and puts her head down.*

*"No, I need help, it's not easy," she cries.*

*Her father shakes his head and walks toward the door.*

*"You need to pull yourself together and focus on this, you can finish it."*

*Lily kicks her feet on the ground and almost growls back at him. Her lips tighten, as she bites down, head buried in her hands.*

*Her father takes a deep breath and squeezes the bridge of his nose.*

*"Lily, just figure it out," he directs as he walks out of the room.*

*She just lies there, not moving. Face in hands, legs sprawled out. The sun fades through the window and the white walls turn to black.*

*Danny stands in the kitchen watching Jenny at the stove. She is stirring ground meat in a pan while skimming through the pile of mail. The bags that held groceries are now empty and stacked neatly on the counter.*

Casey Renee Le'Vasseur

*"How did it go," she asks, sensing him behind her.*
*Danny hangs his head, either in thought or frustration. Jenny*
*turns around to face him when he doesn't respond.*
*"What's wrong?" she pushes.*
*"I dunno. Just another fit," Danny explains.*
*Jenny turns back to the stove and stirs the food in the pan.*
*"Well, she'll be fine," Jenny assures him.*
*"I know, it's just hard to watch," Danny sighs.*

There is no middle ground here, in this moment. The
rage. The anger spilling over in me. The *never good enough's*. So
strong. I was unable to move, slightly foaming at the
mouth. Fists pounding in the ground. It was washing over
me. Making some deal with the devil. *crazy*. I was young. I
was *something's not right*. I was so far from understanding where
it was all coming from.

I was the girl who threw the tantrums. I was the girl always
second guessing. I was the girl afraid of her own shadow. And
at the same time, I was the girl taking over the show, standing
in the spotlight. I was a walking contradiction. I was all over
the place. I was anger. I was elated. I was impulsive, I was
irrational. I was fighting, screaming. I was impossible. I was
so many things I didn't understand. And I was alone, a lot of
the time. I was independent. I was *don't ask for help*. I was
holding on to all the things that went wrong. I was controlled
by this part of myself that I couldn't understand, an extension
of who I was. Me feeling stupid for the mistakes I'd
made. And me not understanding what was happening. And I
knew one day it would make sense, it had to, but that day was
so out of reach. And at that time, in that moment, I thought it
was okay, I thought it was so normal.

12

# Chapter 4

## the fire.

I couldn't have been more than seven. The curiosities, they were inside of me. Typical childhood. Try everything. Do anything. Be anyone. I was fine. Normal. Well adjusted. I was clueless. Carefree. Careless. I was a mess. But I didn't know it then. It was just this growl in the pit of my stomach, this little monster beneath the surface. It was a no name entity, pushing me. Making every thought and action okay. The monster told me to run, so I ran. I remember earlier that day. I remember bits and pieces.

*The family sits in the backyard. The bar-b-que is set up on the driveway, behind the house and Danny is standing over it. Jenny sits on the patio, watching a little baby girl with bright blonde hair rock back and forth in a swing. Lily and Samantha are playing hopscotch on the driveway. A jar of sun tea is brewing on a ledge.*

*Danny takes a couple of burgers from a plate lined in foil and plops them on the grill. He moves them around slightly, then closes the cover and crumbles the foil up on the plate.*

*"Hey girls, check it out," Danny calls.*

*Lily and Samantha turn around and look up at their father. He plays around with the foil and puts the long skinny lighter up to*

13

*it. He holds it there for a few moments before throwing the foil ball on the ground. It makes a little fiery explosion when it hits the ground, then fizzles out.*

*"Woah, how'd you do that?" Samantha questions as she runs over to her father.*

*Playing with a piece of chalk, Lily sits within earshot, watching Samantha and her father.*

*"You have to get a little gas inside of it," Danny explains. "Then you can light it and it makes a little foil bomb."*

*"Cool, can I try?" Samantha questions.*

*Danny shakes his head.*

*"You shouldn't play with fire, just watch."*

*Samantha makes a pouty face, but shrugs it off and heads back over to Lily.*

*"Did you see?" Samantha asks.*

*Lily just traces the lines of the hopscotch. She doesn't look up.*

*"Yeah."*

*Samantha shrugs and calls out to her mom.*

*"Mom, can we drink the tea now?" she shouts.*

*Lily looks over at the bar-b-que. Her eyes lock in tightly on the lighter. She rubs her hand over her ear and shrugs, she pushes her shoulders into her neck, almost as though she is trying to push something away.*

I remember the word freedom whispering in my ear. The day passed on and it grew dark. Everyone busy watching the baby, my new little sister, the little family was growing, and everyone was so busy, busy with homework, busy with life, busy with surviving, busy. I could slip out and disappear and no one would even know. I could get out of there so fast and it wouldn't matter. I didn't know why I wanted to leave. I don't remember anything being wrong. But I remembered the strong scent of hidden memories. Stuffed emotions. Don't talk. Don't tell. Where the restrictions came from, I don't recall. But it felt real. And I suddenly felt alone. And that thing, it let out a huge roar inside of me, and I was gone. Out the door running. Scheming in my mind. I don't even know where the thoughts came from, not me. These thoughts weren't mine. I was happy. I was well adjusted. I was fine. But, before I could stop myself I was in my neighbor's yard. I had a lighter and I was sitting in the grass and all I could feel was fire and all I could think was burn it down. And my brain shut down and it was just me there alone in the dark, something moving my hands, seeing through my eyes, I tried to stop it, but I couldn't. I let it swallow me, devour me inside out. And I was free.

I don't remember much else, there was running home, there was the rush dissipating, there was a feeling like heat washing over my skin and leaving me cold. And then there was my brain turning back on, my eyes finally seeing, my mind spinning stories, accounting for my absence, searching for words to explain away whatever it is I may have done, without even knowing what I was doing. There was the arguing with myself not understanding. And then the monster spoke to me sweetly. And I felt at peace.

*The living room is full of life. Samantha sitting at the desk doing homework, books out, hand writing. Jenny is plopped on the couch breastfeeding Zoe. The TV is on and Danny is skimming through sports scores.*
*Lily is behind the living room wall, in her bedroom. She wiggles her body through the window and falls onto her bed. She recovers and jumps up, quietly closing the window and lying back down on her bed.*
*Back in the living room there is a knock on the front door. Jenny eyes Danny.*
*"What time is it, who is that?" she questions.*
*Danny shrugs.*

*"I dunno, I'll check," he says as he gets up and walks to the door. "It's Neal."*

*Danny opened the door to Neal, the next-door neighbor. He looks frazzled and an air of concern lingers around him.*

*"Is Lily here?" he questions.*

*Danny's forehead scrunches up.*

*"Yeah, why do you ask?" Danny insists.*

*"Do you know where she is?"*

*Danny turns toward the living room. Samantha is working feverishly on her homework.*

*"Jen, where's Lily?"*

*"In her room, reading, I think," she calls out from the couch.*

*"Well, I'm pretty sure I just saw her trying to set my yard on fire. I had to stomp it out."*

*"What? Well that's just absurd. Lily is in her room," he says, almost defensively.*

*"You should talk to her about that," he urges and walks away.*

*Danny closes the door slowly and walks into the living room.*

*Lily is in her room, ear pressed to the door. Her fingers tapping eagerly on the ground. Her shoulders tight as her head moves slowly back and forth. She snaps out of it as she hears her parents walk down the hallway. Lily plops on her bed and fumbles to grab a book. They walk in without knocking.*

*"Lily, did you go somewhere?" Danny questions.*

*Lily looks up from her book at her parents, forcing her body to keep from shaking.*

*"No, where would I go?"*

*"Neal said you tried to light his yard on fire, did you try to do that Lily?" her father pushes.*

*Lily shakes her head.*

*"I'm just reading, I didn't do anything, I promise," she speaks effortlessly.*

*Jenny looks up at the window above Lily's bed. The curtain is ruffled. Her Parents stand there for a moment before walking out the door. They leave it ajar.*

# Chapter 5

## the smoking gun.

There were still peaceful moments with nothing to report. Nothing moments. They were random acts. Random pieces of a story. And all of this was so normal. But the quiet only lasted so long. Then there was the pouting. The crying. The stomping. And it was cute. And they all laughed and my insides came alive and no matter how quiet it was, the sound was deafening. The curiosity pulled at me from time to time.

*Danny slams the side door of the house and stands under the carport. "You can't just walk away," Jenny screams from the other side of the door.*

*Danny stands there with the palms of his hands pressed into his back. He stares aimlessly down the driveway into the road in the quiet neighborhood. Lily peaks her head out of her bedroom window, which sits next to the carport. She watches her dad out the window. He walks to his car, opens the door and reaches inside. When he pulls his arms back out he is gripping a pack of cigarettes. He pulls one out, lights it up, and leans his tired body against the car. He closes his eyes tightly as he inhales the smoke. Everything washing away from the surface, a moment of peace. Lily's tiny head staring at him intently from inside the house.*

I remember sitting outside. Young and curious. Crouched in a corner. I found matches. I found sticks. And I would smoke these little tree limbs. This junk from the ground. Inhale the smoke. Imitation is the highest form of flattery. And that wasn't the last time I'd find myself masking some habit. Strange where I would end up. I remember hearing something calling me so quietly back then, just loud enough to stop me in my tracks, to confuse my actions. To throw me into a fit, stubborn, arguing with myself. And so much still I wasn't aware of at the time. Hindsight catches up with you, opens your eyes. And then there is a flash, everything goes white, and those memories that twisted in you, they disappear too. I fight to get back to those moments, to figure out the meaning and make some sense of the exhaustion. But those moments twist inside of me, and the pieces are so scattered now.

*It's a warm summer day in the suburbs of Chicago. Lily is sitting alone in a tree in the front yard. There is a large moving van in the road outside of the house, two men are loading boxes and furniture inside. Jenny stands on the front porch, Zoe is standing beside her with her little arms wrapped tightly around her mother's leg. Samantha comes running out of the house up to the tree. She climbs it and sits beside Lily.*

*"I'm gonna miss it," Samantha admits.*

*Lily stares at the house and then looks behind her at the moving van.*

*"Something different will be good," Lily suggests.*

*Samantha shrugs and swings her legs back and forth in the air.*

*The Family is piled into a minivan. Danny is driving, Jenny beside him in the front seat. Baby Zoe is in the car seat in the middle and Lily and Samantha are crammed in the back. Lily stares out the window as they drive down a deserted road. The*

*baby lets out a wail. Jenny turns around with a bottle in hand
and passes it Zoe.*
*"Shhh, eat something, and relax," Jenny coos.*
*The noise stops for a moment, but then continues. Growing
louder and louder as they drive down the road. Samantha puts
headphones on her ears and presses play on her walkman. Lily
just sits there, staring into empty space.*

I remember the awkward middle school years. Living in a new
city, a new state, a new place. Those same habits, those voices,
that white noise in the pit of my stomach. I was somewhere
around eleven, and after what seemed like a year hiatus, the
monster came back. I don't know where he went or if he was
ever really gone, or if those moments, those memories are so
fragmented I can't even piece them back together.

*Jenny comes through the garage door carrying a small
suitcase. Behind her a woman with curly, dirty blonde hair, rolls
a larger suitcase and follows her inside.*
*"Girls, Heather is here," Jenny calls out.*
*The floors squeak with movement above their heads. Jenny and
Heather put the bags down and walk into the kitchen. It's open,
with a dining table and French windows revealing a lush green
backyard. The décor is country casual, with antiqued shelving
and gadgets. Heather walks to the door and stares out at the
yard.*
*"It's weird not seeing fences," Heather comments.*
*"I know, I'm still getting use to it," Jenny agrees as she fills up a
glass with water from the fridge. Zoe walks into the kitchen, her
curly blonde ringlets hang in her face.*
*"Hey baby," Heather smiles.*
*Samantha and Lily run into the kitchen and immediately give
Heather a big hug.*

*"Hey, I missed you girls. It's so good to see you."*

*Lily smiles and walks to the pantry. She stares at the shelves for a few minutes before grabbing a box of crackers.*

*"Girls, we're gonna go get some dinner, want to come?" Jenny asks.*

*"I have so much homework, I'm sorry Heather. Can you bring me something home?" Lily says as she runs her hand along Zoe's head.*

*"Sure. You ready to go?" Jenny looks over at Zoe. She is jumping up and down singing and running to the door. Jenny and Heather laugh as they follow behind. Heather stops at her small suitcase before walking out the door. She reaches in her purse and pulls out a small key and unlocks the bag. She unzips it and slides out a pack of Virginia Slims. There are several more left inside. She zips it back up and leaves the house. Lily is standing in the kitchen, staring at the closed door. Her eyes move to the small suitcase tucked in the corner.*

I remember her going out one day with my mom and I picked the lock on her suitcase and grabbed a handful of cigarette packs. I didn't really know what I was going to do with them, I just knew I needed to have them. Needed the rush. I hid them somewhere in my room where no one would find them and spun a million things in my mind. A dizzying web that I couldn't escape from. I kept wanting to put them back, throw them out. I don't even know why I took them, but I had to. Couldn't stop. Needed to feel something. I kept them for a while, sitting in their hiding place, not sure what to do. Time passing, seasons changing, until the bug hit me and I had to act. I had to play it safe, stay hidden, the monster didn't want to be exposed. Didn't want to be found out. And I obeyed. I had no choice.

Early mornings before school, the only one awake. I would find the large Easter egg I kept hidden in my closet. There used to be a chocolate bunny in it, and some fake green grass. Now the paper-mache shell enclosed a pack of Virginia Slims, a lighter, and a pair of latex gloves. Silently moving through the house, I would make my way outside. At a tree behind my neighbor's house, I'd pull out my kit, and like a doctor preparing to see a patient, I would go through my routine. I pulled the latex gloves quickly over my shaking hands, my heart racing. Then in the early of the morning, before the sun even came out, I'd stand there, in the middle of winter, smoking a few Virginia Slims before my morning shower.

# Chapter 6

## sushi.

There are these strange moments that happen. These shifts in the wind. Everything covering over me. There are these paralyzed moments. These stubborn, confused, sensitive, holding back, shutting down moments. And they come on like lightening at the strangest times.

*Danny sits at the kitchen table with a plate of sushi in front of him. The lights are dimmed slightly and the kitchen is spotless except for a stack of children's artwork on the opposite edge of the table. Danny is dressed in khakis and a polo shirt. Jenny walks over to the table from the sink and takes a seat beside him. He mixes bright green wasabi into a small bowl of soy sauce with a pair of chopsticks.*

*"So, what's Japan like?" Jenny questions.*

*Danny pops a sushi roll into his mouth and gives her a thumbs-up. She laughs and nudges him in the arm.*

*"It's been hard here, without you," she admits. Danny puts his hand on hers.*

*"I know I've been gone a lot. I just want to build a good future for you."*

*There is a squeaking upstairs. Danny and Jenny both look up at the ceiling toward the sound.*

*"Looks like we might have some kids awake,"* Danny
deducts. *Jenny and Danny both turn to the doorway, waiting for
their visitors.*

*Lily and Samantha come peaking around the corner.*

*"Hello girls,"* Danny grins *as the two of them walk side by side
into the room.*

*Lily and Samantha are both dressed in pajamas. Their father
motions them to sit down at the table, and they do. Lily folds her
knees into her chest and presses them against the table.*

*Danny takes a sushi roll in his chopsticks and dips it in the soy
sauce. He holds it in front of Samantha.*

*"Want a bite?"* he moves it closer.

*"What is it?"* Samantha questions.

*"Sushi. It's amazing. It's not as good as I had in Japan, but
it's still delicious."*

*"Sure,"* Samantha says as she opens her mouth wide. *Her father
drops the sushi inside. Her eyes open big as she chews it.*

*Lily stares at the plate of sushi, slightly licking the corners of her
lips, barely noticeable.*

*"Lily, I don't know if you'll like it, do you want to try it?"* he
asks her.

*Lily shrugs. She squeezes her hands together beneath the
table. Her eyes locked on the plate of food, her legs pulled tightly
into her chest.*

*Danny takes another bite. Samantha reaches over and grabs
another roll, drenching it in soy sauce before popping it into her
mouth. Lily just stares, her toes twitching beneath the table.*

*"Was Japan fun dad?"* Samantha asks as she dips a finger in
the soy sauce.

*"Ya it was neat. We'll all have to go back sometime."*

Silence & Noise

*The conversation fades into the background as Lily's gaze locks on the pile of drawings at the edge of the table. She closes her eyes tightly.*

Something strange triggered in me. Maybe the conversation. Maybe something in the air. Hard to put my finger on it. I said no. Wanted to say yes. Yes was on the tip of my tongue. I couldn't form the words. Something deep inside of me, covering me from the inside out. It felt like something was crawling all over my skin. I just wanted to scream. I could feel the anger slipping through my lips. Upset. Miserable. I kept telling myself to do something. Say something. But I was stuck. Trapped in the in between and I couldn't get out.

And those moments were increasing. These can't put my finger on it. Have to get out moments. I felt them growing, increasing, and no matter how hard I tried. I couldn't stop it. I couldn't stop them.

# Chapter 7

## an error in judgment.

Twelve and thirteen were somewhat of a blur. There were times when I felt the intensity rising, but there was still a barrier, there was still a part of me that existed. I wasn't completely destroyed. The edges were frayed, but somewhere I was still convinced this would all pass. It would fade. My mind would be clear, and quiet. The weeks and years that I lived through then, intensified. Without my knowledge I found myself lost. Unable to stop. But if I really wanted to I could. That's what I kept telling myself.

It started one day at a store in a nondescript mall. In the middle of a town of people, in a place I didn't feel at home in. I never felt at home. A little cash burning a hole in my pocket. The dollar sign, the price on the tag, not enough. I'd never have enough. I pictured those girls at my school, the ones who had everything. Now as I remember them more clearly, their messy pony tails atop their heads, all in the same clothing, in unison, swapping boyfriends, lipstick, mascara, I get sick. But in that very moment, for just a moment I thought, that could be me. And that was all the monster needed.

*Lily stands in a dressing room. Surrounded by mirrors. Loud, too loud music plays in the background as she stares at herself. Standing in the mirrored room in her own clothing. A stack of clothes hang on a hook on the door. Lily pulls at her shirt, pulls at her arms, closes her eyes so tightly, and shakes her head. Half saying no, half spastic. Her eyes pop open and she sits on a little chair in the corner of the fitting room. She stares at the first shirt hanging in front of her. Lily slowly takes it off the hanger, examines, and stuffs it in her bag. She lays the empty hanger under the chair, grabs the rest of the clothes and marches out of the room. She quickly lays them on the counter.*

*"Thanks," she forces out as she walks slowly, then quickly to the door. Her eyes fixated straight ahead.*

*The store clerk watches her as she walks away. Then Lily is gone, out of the door. Soon enough she has run her way out of the mall doors. Leaving the stark cold building into the heat, the sun burning her skin. Awakening her.*

Free. At last. That's all I needed. That one moment and then I just needed more. More moments. A bigger rush. Something more. From shirts, to lotions, perfumes, anything I could get my hands on. I needed more. Needed to remember that feeling, that feeling of freedom. And it just grew and the sounds got louder and louder until I could barely take it. And then everyone was watching me. They were staring, I couldn't get away from them, couldn't move. Couldn't breathe.

*Lily stands alone in a mall department store. Elevator music playing a little too loudly through the speakers. She wanders around the store. Almost lost, stuck in her head. She doesn't make eye contact as people pass her by, she just follows their shadows behind them. Lily stops in her tracks in front of a set of mannequins. She stares at the coordinated outfit, the fake skin, the pale features. She touches the mannequin's hand and it falls off into hers. She almost jumps back, looks around. No one is there, she is alone. She twists the hand back on, then hesitates before pulling it off again. She scans the room once more before stuffing the hand in her purse. Her heart racing inside of her chest. The corners of her mouth form into a half smile.*

*At school the next day Lily sits at a long table in a big cafeteria. The room is loud around her, a mixture of conversations about boys and sports and homework. The group she is sitting with is discussing the upcoming battle of the bands. Lily is half paying attention. She pulls the pale mannequin hand out of her purse and throws it on the table. She has painted the nails silver with a paint pen. They all turn and stare.*

*"Whoa, what's that from?" a boy asks.*

*Lily shrugs and almost grins. A girl grabs at it.*

*"Is this a mannequin hand?" she questions excitedly.*

*Lily nods and the table roars in laughter and amazement.*

*"Cool." "Let me see it." "I want one, Lily will you get me one?"*

*"You can come with me," Lily shrugs and nods.*

*The table, a little too excited by the prospect. Lily, just watching from the outside.*

I sort of let them into this secret world. I left the door ajar. And then it was gone. The rush. The freedom. It vanished. And I was hungry again.

## Chapter 8

## dirty walls.

I slowly learned that I was the ringleader. I had the ability to hold power and control over someone. It was a subtle, quiet power. A suggestion. A hint. An idea I'd place in their minds. I could do it, because it was happening to me. These thoughts that would haunt me, devour me, suffocate me. I shared those ideas, convincing my friends to go along. One part of me, the part of me studying, excelling, was terrified of what would happen, what my parents would think or say. The other part was black, haunted, and haunting others in return. And it was all I could do to stay afloat.

*Lily and two other girls are standing in a school bathroom. Generic cinderblock walls, painted grey. Lily is wearing jeans and a tight t-shirt, her brown hair framing her petite face and frame. One of the other girls is short and dressed similar to Lily. The other girl is a little more put together, wearing a cute skirt and shirt. They stand around by the mirrors, putting on make-up, washing their hands.*

*Lily stares at the grey wall, drawn in, she walks over to touch it. She runs her hand across its surface. The girls behind her, in the background.*

*"I think he was asking me out, I don't really know," the girl in the skirt shares.*

*"Well, what did he say?" the other girl questions.*

*Lily pulls a bright blue paint pen out of her bag. She shakes it back and forth, the metal ball inside, so loud. She puts the pen to the wall and unleashes a fury of scribbles. Doodles. Abstract art. The pen moving quickly in her hand.*

*The other girls turn around and see Lily's start of a masterpiece.*

*"Oh my god, Lily, what are you doing?" skirt girl urges.*

*Lily looks up and grins, her smile not quite meeting her eyes. She holds the pen out in front of her, toward the other girls. They stare at her for a moment in hesitation. Lily shakes it back and forth so the metal ball is the only sound. The jeans and t-shirt girl grabs it from Lily's hand and starts writing on the wall. Phrases, lyrics. When she finishes, she hands the pen to the other girl and they all stand back and stare at their creation. The three girls walk arm in arm out of the bathroom. Not even stopping to wash the paint off their hands.*

There it was. That thing roaring inside of me, pleased for a moment. Sign your name I thought in that moment, mark it, take credit. The hint of sanity inside of me screamed, pleaded for me to stop, to grab a sponge, to end this. I could see the nervousness in their eyes as we walked away. I wondered if they could see mine or if my eyes were just black, unreadable, I wanted to be invisible. And it all seemed so easy, I convinced myself I could walk away. That we could leave there and it would end there. I displaced it, the memory. Buried it. It never happened.

But that didn't stop it from coming back up, haunting me. There was a meeting. The school, desperate to get to the bottom of it. All three girls, sitting there. Wondering what was going on, why we were there, what was happening. Somehow they deducted it all down to this group of girls, threw us in a room, and let us sweat. My heart pounding, as I allowed myself to remember the events of the last few days. I spun the stories in my head, the lines I would tell, and I didn't even have to think about it. It poured into me and I instructed the girls, and we came to an agreement. We made a plan. And it all came back to get me. I wondered if I could run, if I could get out of there, go back and change it, do it over again. And I went numb. I swallowed my punishment. It didn't matter what they made me do, it was my parent's faces I didn't want to see. I made the grades, kept to myself, I was what they wanted me to be. This would shatter that. Or maybe it would just make me visible.

*Outside of Lily's house it's dark. A few flood lights shine down on a picnic table just outside of the kitchen. The lights are on inside. Zoe is standing there, her face pressed against the French window, making faces. Lily sits at the table in front of her parents. Her mom with her arms across her chest. Lily staring down at the wooden table. Her dad holding down the fort.*

*"Lily, what were you thinking? They could have kicked you out of school! Why would you do this? What did we do wrong?" Danny begs her to answer.*

*Lily shrugs, not looking up.*

*"Look at me when I'm talking Lily."*

*She winces, twitches slightly as she stares at his neck. The closest to eye contact she can make. The noise fades away in the background and she just sits there, staring at their necks as they speak their piece.*

This was getting out of hand. It was too much and I couldn't take it anymore. Something had to change. I had to change. And I could, if I wanted to, I could. I could keep the monster at bay if I forced it down, if I stuffed it away. I had to stop feeding it. It would shrink, and I could go back to being invisible. So I opted for invisibility. After the incident in the girl's locker room, invisibility seemed like my only means to survival.

There were random moments. There was desperation. There was the weight of something dragging inside of me. My body heavy, my mind numb. The only way I could move forward. To pretend the past never happened. To start fresh. My heart, grey black, my eyes heavy. I was dead inside.

# Chapter 9

## chasing down the memories.

Now feeling like I had somehow been exposed. A part of my secret revealed. Not knowing where to go from here. Or how to get back. Things had changed so quickly from those days when I was young, building sandcastles. Making mud pies. Thinking the buzzing in my ears was normal. Never noticing the big things. My mind set on the tiny things. The little moments. The difference in the memories is my mind, the part in me wanting to see the good. Wanting to remember the moments that were light, free. My mind can't get there. It can't go back to that. I try to find the goodness in the mess. I try to remember the laughing. The jokes. And the part of me, in the deepest part of me, that can't see it. It can't get out of the darkness and see the smiles. No matter how much I force it, try to drag it there, it is just darkness. It is only black. And time so quickly changed. What was once innocence became a pool of darkness. It was me wanting to burn it all down. And there had to be moments of joy. There had to be these memories of my parents, before it all set in, before everything got so hard.

*Danny and Jenny sit on a blanket on the grass outside of their home. Lily and Samantha run around an above ground pool, chasing each other. Lily pauses for a moment, back pressed up against the flimsy pool siding, watching her parents. It's late afternoon and the sun is just starting to set above their little home. Danny and Jenny, fingers intertwined, watch the clouds take shape. Samantha tosses a beach ball in Lily's direction, stirring her from her daydream.*

But I can't find them. Can't hold on to them. I would try to retrace them when things were really bad. In the deepest depths of the grave I would try to find those quiet moments. And they were gone. They had vanished. And even now, with some sense of clarity in my thoughts, as I search for them. Some so deeply buried they are faded. They are worn down. And so many other moments, so out of reach. No matter how hard I try to grasp them. I can't wrap my fingers around them. The more I try, the more I slip up, recreate a scene of events. These stories I tell myself to pretend it is all okay. I find those things. And they become my memories. These new stories I can keep in the back of my mind. But as time passes, I lose myself in all of this. And I hate it. I hate how faded all of it has become. I hate how quickly I lost it all. How far away it all is. I hate knowing I may never get those moments back. I hate knowing the black has covered over me so much. The result of so much pushing, pulling, shoving. So much of me trying to squash the thoughts, the pain inside of me. I numbed myself so much from everything. But it never stopped the pain. It just filled my brain with emptiness. My thoughts so distant and the pain still building inside of me. The loss of innocence. The loss of thought. I wanted to pull those things back. And I couldn't. They were gone.

## Chapter 10

# the relationship fix.

I had an idea. A way to pour myself into something else. A sort of negotiation with myself, an agreement, some middle ground. I could use normal stimulus, the things people my age were supposed to concern themselves with. I was supposed to be overjoyed to have a boyfriend. To go on dates, to hold hands. To talk on the phone late at night, in a whisper so no one heard. To sit in silence, just breathing to each other. I could do that. I could be that girl.

Slowly I allowed myself to feel something again. Little bits of it. Moments of some happiness. The rush of hands brushing each other accidentally. And I felt okay inside. It wasn't the same as the moments before; running thru the mall, the art, the lies, it was a different rush. It felt mild but I convinced myself it was enough and it had to be better than the weight I was carrying inside. The loud roars I struggled to keep at bay.

I was thirteen and in love, because I figured I was supposed to love this boy. My first boyfriend. It was innocent, and then it was more because I foolishly thought this could be enough. But I grew weary and tired. Catering to someone else's emotions when my insides were running around, screaming to get out. He was sweet, and kind, and crazy over me. And I told myself to mirror him, to feel what he felt, this emotion, this passion, this intensity that radiated from his flesh. I could be that, I could feel that. But it was a lie, because I couldn't. I thought maybe he was lying, maybe it was some dreamworld people created to convince us that it was possible to feel so much. But it was real for him, and genuine, and I was incapable of feeling anymore.

*Lily stands in a school hallway getting books from her locker. A bright eyed boy approaches her. He slips a folded up piece of paper from his front pocket into her open locker and casually walks away. Lily's heart races a little as she turns to see him walking backward down the hallway, grinning big.*

The rush I remembered at the beginning faded quickly. And the idea of working at it seemed exhausting. So I pulled back. I pushed the monster back down into the pit of my stomach to shut it up. It kept screaming for more. But I just felt numb. I couldn't feel it anymore. So I walked away.

Then I found myself wondering if I could keep those first moments. The times when the rush would cover my body and I could feel it all for a moment. I wanted that, I wanted to keep it in a bottle and use it when I needed it. Use it when I felt that pressure inside, when the weight got too heavy. So I forced myself to play the game, trying to trick myself into feeling something. Flirting, daydreaming, lingering eyes, playful jokes, leading them on. The attention was intoxicating. And it felt like it was working, and I believed I could end it. I could finally solve the problem and be free. I could satisfy the monster with these little moments. And before I could stop it, my obsession with love began. The story of the girl looking for an escape. Were forced emotions still emotions?

*Part II*

# Chapter 11

## the awakening.

There was a comfort in realizing things could slow down. I could find a quick fix, a solution, it didn't have to be so hard all of the time. I savored those moments. The times when there was peace and quiet and I didn't need to worry. It was all so calm. But those in betweens were never permanent, and when I finally started to think I had a hold of it, I lost my tight grip and it all slipped out from under me. I made believe it was the boy. The boy of the moment I decided to pour myself into. Little obsessions, little moments. Fairytales. I had it all planned out in my mind, and I lost it. I wasn't the right girl. And there it was again. Those thoughts, those feelings gnawing inside of me. *You're never enough. You'll never be good enough.* And it was almost funny that I thought I could be the girl who got the guy. The irony is, I was the girl that got the guy a lot of the time, but I couldn't see that then, and I'm getting ahead of myself. And those thoughts, they twisted inside of me. And I knew then, what I had thought for so long. I wasn't good enough.

So the guy, the crush of the moment, Dylan, or no, I think it was David, something I erased, he got the girl, my best friend at the time. And I played like it didn't matter. But I remember when he was almost mine.

*A small cottage of a home, slightly tattered around the edges out in the middle of nowhere. School has ended for the summer, a celebration of sorts. A small gathering. Lily and Samantha sit outside with a group of people. Lily wears jeans and a bright pink belly shirt. She watches Samantha as she talks with a group of people, a mixture of gutter punk and hippie.*

*"Jello Biafra is amazing, I don't care what you say," Samantha exclaims.*

*Lily plays with rocks on the ground, rolling them back and forth in her hands. After a while she looks up. A boy, dressed in slightly baggy corduroy pants, a white t-shirt, and Etnie tennis shoes strums a guitar as he leans against the windowsill. Another boy with a bright red Mohawk leans on the house beside him. Lily's eyes lock on the guitar boy.*

*Later a group of them are crowded on the floor in a tiny bathroom. Most of them are smoking cigarettes and a stereo is playing in the background. Lily is pressed up close to the guitar boy. She pokes him with her finger.*

*"Hey, sorry I'm kinda squashing you," she smiles coyly.*

*"I don't mind," he smiles back at her.*

*"How is your summer going so far?" she questions.*

*Someone hits the light switch and the room goes black. A roar of laughter ignites the room.*

*"What the hell, where's the light?" someone screams in the darkness.*

*"It's kinda nice, keep it off," another answers back.*

*The glow of cigarettes is the only light in the room. The back and forth conversations continue in the background. The guitar boy leans in closer to Lily.*

*"Summer is good so far," he whispers in her ear, his warm breath igniting her senses. So close to her face she can almost feel his lips touch her ear. Lily takes his hand and intertwines it in hers. He*

*doesn't pull away and she moves his hand to her breasts. She holds it there, the heat of her body and his. A room full of people, fire radiating between them. Suddenly without warning the light flashes back on and he quickly pulls his hand away. She looks over and smiles as she stands up and files out of the bathroom with everyone else. Leaving him stunned, on the floor.*

*Lily passes the Mohawk boy in the corner on her way into the living room. She plops down on a big couch. Operation Ivy plays in the background as she lies down with her eyes closed.*

*"Hey," the guitar boy says as he sits down beside her.*

*Lily pops her eyes open and looks up at him. He is perfect.*

*"You know I like you," she admits.*

*"Yeah I know."*

*She picks at his corduroy pants, they are worn around the edges.*

*"Kelly likes you too," she adds.*

*He looks down, away from her.*

*"I know."*

*"Are you choosing her?" Lily questions.*

*He doesn't look up as he speaks.*

*"It's complicated."*

*Lily rolls on her side.*

*"It's always complicated."*

*He touches her arm gently, closing his eyes as his fingers trace her skin. Softly, slowly, she removes his hand from her.*

*"You can't do that, you can't touch me. You can't have it both ways."*

*He nods as he gets up and walks away. Lily lies there, eyes closed, music fading into the background.*

I folded my hands and congratulated Kelly on her relationship, on her victory. Like it was some kind of competition, some race to the finish. I really was happy for her, but what ate away at me was the constant feeling of inadequacy.

*Lily lies on the bottom bunk bed in her pale green bedroom. She holds a purple cordless telephone between her ear and the bend in her neck.*

*"Kelly, really, it's not a big deal," Lily assures her.*

*"Well, I just want you to be happy, to find someone," Kelly says from the other end of the line. Lying somewhere on a bed with her perfect blonde hair, perfect skin, perfect life.*

*"David and I were thinking maybe you and Seth would make a cute couple," Kelly suggested.*

*Lily was silent, fidgeting around on her bed.*

*"He's so cute, and you both have brown eyes, and isn't his Mohawk cute, and I don't know, you guys would get along," Kelly insists.*

*"I don't really know him, I don't even have his number, that's just weird."*

*"I'll give you his number, just call him. I think he might like you."*

*Lily hangs up the phone and walks to her closet. She peeks into the corner and traces her fingers along the initials D.P.M. drawn in black pen on her closet wall. She closes her eyes, sits down in the tiny closet, turns the closet light off, and shuts the door.*

Not only did I fail, but I couldn't get that damn voice to turn off, and just when I thought I had all of this under control. And this wouldn't be the last time. I was ready for the next chapter. High school. So I took my consultation prize. The friend of the boy I wanted to be my boy. His name was Seth, and he was a boy in a band.

*Lily sits in the dark of the closet, a light up telephone in her hands.*

*"So, hi, Kelly gave me your number. She thinks we should be friends I guess," Lily explains.*

*"Yeah, David too," Seth adds.*

*Seth is pacing around a small apartment on the other side of town. His un-spiked Mohawk messy. His t-shirt covered in black sharpie writing.*

*"So should we?" Lily questions.*

*"What?"*

*"Be friends?"*

*"Yes, we should," Seth smiles and leans up against a wall in his apartment. His eyes close softly.*

*Lily in her closet, closes her eyes too, a soft smile across her face.*

He was way more than a boy in a band. Even though it wasn't what I thought I wanted, in a way I got the better end of the deal. Because the emptiness inside, it found some comfort. This boy, he was a good one. But that was a problem, a big problem, because at that time, in those moments, this would not work. Me, the girl physically and emotionally incapable of forming any true bond with another person. If they saw me, knew me for me, what was inside, this terror in the pit of my stomach. This creature, waiting for an escape, a release, anything. I couldn't expose that. So I would keep myself at a distance, I had to.

And that was Seth and me. Some twisted balancing act between a relationship and a friendship. It was a tightrope walk and I was losing my balance. Every time I wanted to catapult this thing into something more, I fought it. Even though the screaming inside, the demanding was getting louder and louder, I forced it silent. Because this boy, he was a really good one. I didn't want another disaster. I didn't want to go numb. I didn't want to lose whatever it was we had in those moments. And maybe he was empty inside like me, and maybe he needed this too.

*Seth sits on the bed in his room. White walls covered in band posters and show fliers. He holds up a cordless phone and places it on the bedside table. He sits here for a moment with his head in his hands, before rising and walking to a corkboard on the wall. A little picture of Lily is displayed with a push pin. She is standing by the ocean with a flower in her hair, smiling.*

But I couldn't, I wouldn't give in, because I wanted to keep him. I wanted to keep those perfect innocent moments. Those long phone calls. Those silent looks. Those stupid fights and frustrations. I wanted to keep them in a box in my mind, and I wanted to keep him there, because I wanted him safe from the monster. But I was losing it. And I needed more.

## Chapter 12

## *it was one for the books.*

It was summer in the south. It was scorching heat. It was short shorts and midriffs. It was neighborhood pools and picnics. It was too much, and not enough. It was best friends. It was the excitement of going to high school and it was the in between. I remember the lazy days. Sitting by the pool, me and my best friend Kelly (the one who got the boy) in matching swimsuits. Our biggest problem was what we'd wear to our friend's party that night. The biggest problem, I made myself believe. I was second guessing. And I was, *is everything ok with me* confused. I was never knowing when the ball would drop. I was juggling my emotions, and I was doing it all with a smile. At least some of the time. Less of the time. I was losing time.

I remember the boys. I remember us flirting. Me doing stupid things to get their attention. It was late night. It was slumber parties at my friends, sneaking out to spend time with the neighborhood boys. It was smoking my first joint with the boys. I was curious and I wanted to be a part of something, I wanted to belong somewhere, and I wanted to feel something other than numb.

> *Lily and a group of friend sat in a circle in a dark corner of a cul-de-sac. She and her best friend Kelly are the only girls there and*

49

*Kelly is anxiously looking around. The guys are passing a joint around the circle and when it makes its way to Lily she slowly pulls it up to her lips, wraps them softly around it as the guys chat about some CD that just came out. After Lily takes a couple puffs of the joint, the groups walks down to the neighborhood playground.*

*Lily watches out of the corner of her eye while Kelly flirts with her boyfriend. She is unaware of the group of guys staring at her, looking her up and down. She closes her eyes and lies back on the merry-go-round. One of the boys, dark brown hair, intense eyes, slowly spins it around. Lily reaches her hands above her head, the breeze igniting her skin, the corners of her shirt blowing up to reveal her flesh. The guys turn and stare.*

*Lily keeps her eyes closed, a soft smile on her lips, and she lies there as the world spins around.*

Me wanting to be noticed. Me wanting to forget about my thoughts. This was me being normal. Me fitting in, me thinking so much, trying not to think, never wanting to think. And that summer, we let the sun burn our skin, as we talked about high school, boys and being a grownup one day. I wanted that freedom, but I was scared of letting go. I was hoping high school, getting older, all of these life experiences would change me. I wanted them to open me up and take the bad out. I wanted them to fix me.

The maturity process of the disease is not growing out of it, it's accepting it, it is dealing with it as it is, and trying to not let it destroy you. But then, in those moments, it was clouded by teenage drama. By boys, by friends, by school. It was me living with the weight on top of everything else. It was me not understanding how everyone else could walk around so happy. So carefree. Little reservations. It was me trying to discover some meaning in the madness. And as always, it was me believing time would heal me. That high school would heal me. That a boyfriend would heal me. I truly believed it then, that summer. When life was as simple as it was going to get. When I had the thought process to sit and think through it. To understand the differences between then and now, and the loss of innocence. I wanted to cling on to something good in me, but this dark cloud was creeping inside of me, it was laughing at me. It was yelling at people. It was saying without thinking. It was *can't stop.* It was *go away.* It was *I'm up for anything.* All these things that people say, it's good to be bold, good to be daring, good to take chances. Risks. All of these were supposed to be good things. But why was my mind spinning? Why was I losing consciousness? Why was I here?

*Chapter 13*

*this will do.*

High school. That meant change, I thought, and I couldn't get there fast enough. I convinced myself everything would be different, and I was pretty dead on, but not quite the way I expected. I was the new girl, and this could be good. Things started out nicely, with my sister, Sam already established at the school, it made the transition a lot easier. I already had a group of friends to hang out with, and there was a security in that. And they were older, which put me ahead of the rest of the freshman class. I spent my weekends with friends, at shows, listening to music and hanging out. Seth and I stayed friends, or whatever we were. All I know is when someone asked me "if you could marry anyone right now who would it be?", I didn't have to think about it. But I'm pretty sure now that he didn't know, and I know it's probably because I stuffed it, fought it, and ran from it.

Since I couldn't have him, couldn't go there, I let my mind move on. The replacement was a few years older, and totally smitten with me. His name was Mark, he was blonde and he played guitar in a punk band. It was nice to have the attention, to have someone crazy about you, it felt good. For a while. I split my time between him, and friends, and Seth, who had my heart. The more time I spent with Mark, the new boyfriend, the harder he fell. I tried to fall too. I tried to release myself, let go, and give in to it. If he could feel so strong, maybe I could too. Maybe we could just be, in love, and I could be happy. But I was young and I was far from happy, and I was exhausted. I just wanted to scream, scream so loud it would burst my own eardrums. I wanted to jump off the highest building and land on my feet and run some more. And then, his love became too much. It was obsessive, it was over protective. It wasn't fun and I needed fun. I needed light. I needed flirtation. I couldn't do serious. I couldn't release myself enough, to get close to someone like that, and the pressure was killing me. If I hid the insanity, maybe I could keep my sanity. It didn't make sense but I tried it, and I was failing.

The more he fell for me, the more I had to run. And I ran, to Seth, the boy I wanted so desperately to love. And I hated myself for it, because I knew in my heart I needed him, somehow I convinced myself Seth could fix it and he could make it better and I could fix him too. He was quiet, sweet, never spoke up, never too serious, but something was bubbling beneath the surface. But the moment I realized he could love me too, I stopped. Scared of my own shadow. The idea of love truly being reciprocated scared the hell out of me. I remember the very moment.

*Seth, at his dad's apartment in the middle of the afternoon. He sits on his bed, while Lily, on the floor looks through photos.*

*"What time is your mom getting you?" he questioned*

*Lily shrugs, not looking up. Seth just stares at her. She is unaware, she is anxious for no reason, she is moody, inattentive. She stops on a photo of Seth and her. Outside of a club, his arm around her, big smiles on their faces. She looks up at him.*

*"Can I have this?"*

*"Let me see it," he reaches toward the photo.*

*Lily gets up and stands in front of him holding out the photo with both hands. He takes the photo and stares at it for a moment. He puts it down on the bed and reaches his arms up to her hips. He wraps his hands gently around them and looks up at her. She just stands there, not moving, her heart racing, her mind spinning. She wants this, wants to be near him, so close she can't tell where she ends and he begins, it's all she can think about as his dark, sad, lonely eyes stare up at her. He pulls her in, pulls her closer as he sits there on the bed, as she stands tall before him. He rests his head on her stomach, and breathes in deep. Her hands twitch as she imagines running them through his hair. But this can't happen, there is still Mark, and there is still the monster inside, and there is still her holding back. She gently pushes him away.*

*"We can't, I'm sorry," she explains.*

And I walked away. I walked away and I could feel his heart drop and I could hear the sound of it shattering as I walked out the door. And it was so loud it echoed. And then I realized, my heart shattered too. Part of me wanted to run to my boyfriend, break it off, leave it, and then run back here and just be. Just feel, just live, stop running, slow it down and let go. But I couldn't. The idea of someone seeing the monster inside of me was terrifying, and I didn't want to, couldn't live with myself putting Seth through that, putting him through the mess I was.

I was a terrible person; I was unlovable because I was incapable of loving back. It was a selfish way to live. Letting someone fall and running away, letting them hit the ground. But I couldn't connect with that feeling then, and I still barely understand it now. I fought inside myself, with myself to get to that moment back in that room, in that apartment, but I couldn't get there. I couldn't find a way there. I lost it and it was gone.

I did eventually end the relationship with Mark, the one that filled the space and time. It went too fast too far and he was too deep in it. I had been slowly developing this disdain for him over the course of the months we spent together. His love made me nauseous. Couldn't look at him anymore, don't *touch me, kiss me, feel for me.* I wanted to shout, but instead I pushed away, pulled back, and vanished emotionally. Not that I was all there emotionally to begin with. But it had to end, I needed to move on. A secret part of me imagined if I ended it, I could be with Seth, have what I really wanted, needed. Nothing ever works out the way you'd hope. But I was in the driver's seat, so the only person I could blame was me.

*Chapter 14*

*the first cut.*

I'm getting out of order here, but that's okay. There are some things we push so deep inside we don't want to get there, we don't want to face them. This was one of those things. And I'm not proud of this, but there is a lot I'm not really proud of.

I remember the day, I was sitting in some cramped classroom, over analyzing some aspect of a relationship gone wrong, and it hit me. Like a Mack truck. I knew this feeling, I knew this pain all too well. This overwhelming uproar inside of me. I fought to keep my mouth shut. I grabbed my skin on my left arm tightly with my right hand. My nails, like claws deep in my flesh. I held it there for a few moments, numb now, forgetting about the insides, forgetting about the pain, content for a moment. It was then I realized I had another way, something besides these intense moments, this fighting for more, an adventure, a distraction. Now I had a better defense mechanism. This was good. This was perfect. This was what I had been looking for. I thought this was what I needed.

When I finally released my hand the sting of the absence of pressure rushed over me. And I smiled, because I loved it. As the days passed, as the hours grew harder, and the pressure increased, this was my escape. I had this now.

I was sitting at home in my room, the noise of the house suffocating me. The screaming, the fighting, the blaming. My older sister in some shouting match with my parents. My little sister, sobbing. I needed that silence again, I needed it all to shut off. I ripped into my arm with my nails, it stung at first, but it slowly subsided, and there was peace and quiet. I forgot about everything surrounding me and vanished for a moment into this quiet space. I liked this, this was good. As the time lapsed and I forgot about all the things I needed to do, I woke up from the unconscious state and released my grip. School, papers, work, study, phone calls, everything rushed over me at once and there I was again paralyzed by these things, this task list in me. I shook it away and stood up from my desk. Stepping back to think for a moment, to see if I could get the focus back, the peace. It was fruitless, but I plowed forward and tackled the stack of homework on my desk. It was all pretty basic once I dove in, I could handle this, do this. This was easy. I was okay. I looked back down at my arm and the nail marks, the blood clotting, filling in the gaps. Then it hit me, how would I hide this, what was I supposed to do? A momentary freak out. Guilty, ashamed, then numb. Nothing. Empty. Then I grabbed a hoodie and threw it on, covering the wound, and I went downstairs to face the world. To face my nightmare.

It continued for a while, just like that. When I couldn't take it anymore, this was my salvation, but pretty soon, it wasn't enough anymore. I needed more.

*Lily is sitting at the kitchen table, eating a plate full of bagel bites and pizza rolls. She is staring out the window when her mom walks into the room.*
*"Did you finish your homework?"*
*Lily pops a pizza roll in her mouth, eyes focused on a squirrel running around in the yard.*

*Her mom shakes her head as she cleans up a pile of crumbs surrounding the toaster oven.*

*"You shouldn't eat so many of those," she mumbles under her breath.*

*Lily rolls her eyes as Zoe and a friend run into the kitchen, screaming.*

*"Mom, she broke my doll," Zoe screams as she drags her doll behind her.*

*Lily cringes as Zoe wails. She leaves her plate of food and walks upstairs. She plops down on her bed, and roughly massages her temples.*

*She runs into the bathroom, turns on the water in the shower full blast and strips down. She climbs inside and sits cross-legged on the shower floor. Naked and alone. Grabbing the razor from the ledge beside her she stares at it intently. She runs the sharp edge across her skin, and winces slightly. A small stream of blood flows from the surface wound and she closes her eyes, nothing but the sound of water enveloping her.*

*Chapter 15*

*saving lives.*

The next few months went a lot like this. The cuts moved up near my shoulder so they could be covered with a t-shirt. Anywhere else was too risky, too many questions. I didn't need questions. Everything was different, or I imagined it was because I wanted that so bad. But instead of worrying about the boyfriend I couldn't bring myself to love or really care for, instead of dwelling on my heart tearing in two, the more I stuffed my feelings away for someone else, the more I just poured myself into homework, classes, pseudo-friendships. Me perpetually stuck in the joy of acquaintances. Never a need to get close. Always a safe distance. But I remember getting found out, and the fear and the confusion, and the comfort.

It was the last class of the day. Physical education, wellness, some crap class you had to dress out for, it sucked being a freshman. But at least it was the last class of the day, and then it was over. That's where I met him, this kid, Luke. This screwed up kid, more messed up than me. But he didn't hide it, his face read some sob story about a kid, so miserable, so alone. He wore Marilyn Manson t-shirts and painted his nails black, black eyeliner smudged over his eyes. But in here, in this class, we were all sort of the same. Our school uniform fitness clothes. His bleached blonde hair and the black, anywhere he could get it. We became quick friends, we would walk the track together at the end of the day, talking about random stuff, and dreading this class. But there was a little comfort in going there at the end of the day, knowing there was someone else crazy around here. One afternoon I noticed the scars on Luke's arm, and instead of ignoring them, I just blurted it out. I asked him if he cut himself, and he fumbled an excuse. I called him on it because I could sense the truth, I knew that look, I felt it deep inside of myself. And I opened the floodgates. I released what he had been needing to say. And soon enough I was Luke's mentor, his person. We'd spend our afternoons walking the track and analyzing the pains of the moment. He couldn't quite put his finger on it, but he knew he was hurting and he knew he didn't want to be alive. And it made me sad, to think of him there, alone, in his room, hating himself, and desperately wanting to die. I felt his pain, because I knew his pain. Maybe not the exact thing he was feeling, but here was someone, not afraid to say it, not afraid to say he was dying inside. And I loved him for it. Not in the "in love" way, but in the "I wish I could save him and somehow save myself" sort of way. Then he saw it. A scar on my arm from a few days before. Some scab healing itself, stupidly, not knowing it would be reopened soon. He saw it and he asked about it, and I said it was a scratch, a tree branch I walked into. I wasn't as bold as him, I wasn't ready to be saved, or understood. I'm pretty sure he saw through the lie, and that was confirmed later, but I wasn't ready. Not yet.

We started talking online after school. The true age of AOL, instant messaging. The way emotionally void people have dreamed up to communicate. That's when our friendship grew. And that's when he fell in love.

*Lily sits at a desk in front of her computer. An instant message window opens in the center of the screen. She types intently and sits, waiting for a response.*

*Luke, in his house on the other side of town, eyes red from tears, sits in a dark room. Marilyn Mason blaring through the speakers, a bottle of pills and alcohol at his side.*

He was so vulnerable, so alone, and I wanted to help him. But I didn't love him. Not even close. I wasn't what he needed even though he thought I was. I couldn't fix him, but I tried to save him anyway. He talked about all the drugs, all the experimentation, and all the hard stuff he used to numb himself, to fix it. And I would listen and comment, and try to guide him, help him, something. I did what I could, when I could, but it wasn't enough. I couldn't do this full time. He wasn't the guy I wanted to be with, I couldn't even imagine it. But pretty soon it was all he talked about. In between the suicide talk, it was his love, and then it was the love making him want to die, or the love keeping him alive. It was back and forth, up and down. It was him drugged out, typing. It was me telling him to call 911, trying to find out if he was really serious. It was disgusting, but I was captivated, I couldn't turn away. I needed this. He wanted more from me, he needed more, and I refused to give it to him. He begged for a chance, an opportunity to change my mind, and I just couldn't. I was in the middle, or at the end of my relationship with Mark, or who knows, I may have been out of it by this point, but most of it is a blur. We could be friends this way, but that was it. Not me and this guy, I loved his misery, because it made my misery okay to feel. What a disaster this was going to be, but I didn't want to think about that then.

*Luke and Lily sit on the bleachers in the football field at their school. The rest of the class is spread out around them. Luke and Lily in their own world. Some dark cloud hovering over them.*
*"So, when did you start?" he questions her.*

*Lily looks slightly bewildered as he reaches out and touches her shoulder. It's covered in a t-shirt but a fresh wound is beneath the surface. Lily winces slightly from his touch, allowing his hand to sit there for a moment on the wound, a shed of vulnerability leaking through her stony exterior.*

He was the first person I admitted the cutting to. It felt safe because I knew he got it. It was different, what we went through, but he understood the need to feel when you are numb. And if it was this stinging pain, it was still something. At that point, the numbness was getting worse. I had stuffed so many emotions, so many feelings inside and I was losing it. I felt nothing, and at that time I really believed I was nothing. I went through the motions. Got the grades, held conversations, but inside, I was empty. I was nothing.

But once Luke knew my secret, it all became too much. His feelings intensified almost to the point of obsession, and I couldn't do it anymore. Realizing too late I could not help him. If I couldn't be with him, couldn't commit to giving him a chance, I had to walk away. I had to spare him, and I had to save myself. It was exhausting, saving someone's life every day. This was too much for me. Too much for anyone.

Another broken heart. Another left in the dust. But I felt nothing. He tried to win me over, wrote these long notes that he would hand me between classes, they pulled at my heart strings, the fact that someone could love me so much it terrified me. But I felt nothing.

# Chapter 16

## coming clean.

Once I walked away from the dysfunctional friendship with Luke I quickly realized I was alone again. No one really knew what I was facing, battling, hiding. I didn't think I wanted anyone to, but at the same time, there was some comfort in the realness I felt before, with him. In those ridiculous IM conversations, those shameful walks on the track, the bleachers, where I was found out and I couldn't hide it anymore. It was nice to be invisible again emotionally, but there was a void, and I needed to get it out. Needed to come clean. It didn't fix it, change it, or help it, but it was something. I needed something. Mostly I'd just try to distract myself with random moments. I forged friendships to occupy the lost time, and I searched for the next mental fix.

One of my closest friends at the time Clara, was starting to notice the changes in me. It's funny though, because these things were there, always lingering inside. I had carried them with me for so long now, and finally I was showing some wear. I tried to hide it as much as I could, but there wasn't much more I could do. No mask could cover where this was going.

*Clara, a tall redhead eccentrically dressed walks up to Lily in a crowded school hallway. She hands Lily a note, staring intently*

65

*at her for a moment, her eyes sad almost. Lily's heart speeds up
beneath the surface.*

*Lily slides into the closest bathroom. It's empty and she makes
her way into one of the stalls. She sits down, fully clothed on the
toilet seat, pulling out the folded note from her pocket. Her heart
racing, her hands almost trembling as her eyes scan the pages. A
rush of heat covering her skin.*

*"I'm worried about you."*

*"I noticed scars on your arms."*

*Clara's words scribbled out across the page. Her
concern. Urging Lily to get help. Lily, in a daze in the
bathroom stall. Her world collapsing around her.*

I finally worked up the nerve to talk to Clara, tried to spin a
story, think of excuses, but there was no point. No point in
hiding it anymore. But the thing was, now that I let it out to
her, it only got worse. Things didn't change, they just
progressed. I found better ways to cut, better tools, better
spots, better means of disguise. But I didn't stop. She tried to
convince me, tried to tell me, but I couldn't hear her. Couldn't
listen.

At home it was a mess. My dad was busy with a new job, with
deadlines, my mom was busy with us kids, obligations, my older
sister was busy screaming at my parents, and I was busy
slipping away. Lying on my bed listening to the yelling,
witnessing the fistfights, the running out, the slamming doors,
Zoe whining. And it was so easy to silence it.

But, Clara, she said, "I think you need help." And then she
said, "You should talk to him about it."

Him, he was the boy, Seth, the boy I loved. He lived down the
street from Clara and even though we all still hung out alot,
things hadn't been the same between Seth and me. Not since
that one day, not since I broke it off with Mark but still stayed
away from Seth. Finally when I was free, when I could be with

him, and we could finally begin this thing that had been starting and stopping for so long, we just didn't. I hid it away, and I avoided him. Even when we would all hang out, I would fight it. And we would fight, him and me. Not screaming fights, but these strange tug-o-wars, all these feelings, these emotions pouring out and nowhere to put them.

*Seth and Lily sit with a small group of friends in Clara's bedroom. Some group conversation was taking place about what to eat for lunch, and Seth and Lily are almost in the background. They sit at a distance, each stealing glances as the other looks away.*

*"I think my mom made some dip," Clara stood up and motioned the others to follow her to the kitchen.*

*Lily hangs back. As Seth gets up he throws a rolled up ball of paper at her.*

*"What the hell," she shouts as she grabs the paper and throws it back at him.*

*He leaps toward her, almost wrestling her. She bites down on his arm and he screams. They attack each other back and forth. More sexual frustration than fighting. A mixture of playful and angry. Emotions wild beneath the surface.*

That is what we had become. And Clara wanted me to tell him? Talk to him? Confide in him? I was terrified. I didn't know what it would change or fix or why it even mattered. But I sort of had this feeling that despite my relationships and distractions, everyone else around us saw this raging love begging to be unveiled, and everyone was watching, waiting for us to make a move, waiting. And me pretending it didn't matter and acting as though this didn't exist. Then why was I so terrified? If it was nothing, then I should feel nothing, but I didn't, I felt everything.

Somehow I decided to go through with it, decided to talk to Seth, and just get this off my chest. I needed a second opinion, but more than anything I think I needed to know that he could handle this. I needed to hear him, see him, and know if he loved me still. I think the fear came from knowing that if he couldn't handle this, if he walked away, everything inside of me would die, because I held this place for him in my heart and I didn't want to lose that.

*It's a beautiful autumn day. The leaves yellow and orange, and red covering the trees. Clara's yard is covered in a light dusting of leaves. Lily and Clara sit on the front porch drinking sweet tea.*
*"You can do this," she encourages.*
*Lily stares down the street, a longing in her eyes mixed with fear, until Seth comes into view. Her heart thudding inside her chest.*
*"It's gonna be fine," Clara nudged her.*
*Seth walked up to the house and waved at the girls.*
*"What's up?" he questioned.*
*Lily shrugs and Clara stares at her intently.*
*"Not much, how was school?" she forces out.*
*Seth shrugs and walks toward the door. The girls get up and follow him inside.*
*"Need a drink or anything?" Clara offered.*
*Seth shrugs.*
*"I'll see what we have, I'll be back," Clara motions at Lily as she walks into the kitchen.*
*Lily and Seth just stand there in the hallway, avoiding eye contact.*
*"Hey, uh, can I talk to you for a minute?" Lily says almost trembling.*
*Seth just stares at her and nods. He follows Lily into a room by the front door and she closes the door behind them. He sits down*

*on the twin bed and she pulls a chair up beside him. They sit there in silence, her looking down, his eyes on her.*

*"So," he started.*

*"I have a problem," she doesn't move, doesn't look up as she speaks.*

*He waits for her to say more.*

*"I've been, well I'm just not happy, I don't know I think something is wrong."*

*He watches her as she speaks.*

*"I just I think I might need help or something. I don't know I just don't feel right and well," she stopped.*

*"You'll be okay, I mean…"*

*"I cut myself," she blurts out.*

*His eyes widen and his lips tighten on his face.*

*"I mean, a lot, all the time. I don't know why, I just do, and I don't know. Clara says I need help and I don't know if I do. It's probably not that big of a deal. It's probably nothing." She's back peddling.*

*Seth just stares at her, his body frozen, his hands so close to her. His fingers just out of reach. He wants to touch her, wants to hold her. He just sits there as she spins herself into a web.*

A tangled mess of words. *I'm numb, I'm empty, I'm not okay, this isn't okay, and these things I do, they aren't okay.* There was probably a much better word than *okay*, but it was all I could think of. I watched his face drop, without really moving. I guess it was his eyes that sort of fell apart and pretended to be okay with what I was saying. I could see the conflict in his face. I just kept rambling about needing help, needing to talk to my parents but not wanting to, needing to feel, not wanting to be numb anymore. I was so tired of feeling nothing. And I told him I didn't know why I was telling him any of this, but I just wanted him to know, I just needed him to know, and I couldn't explain it. And I don't remember much else. I wanted it to be this magical moment, this time when he would come and save me and fix me and protect me and care for me and never leave me. But I just remember silence, I remember sadness, but I'm pretty sure I interpreted it as something negative. Him hating me, him annoyed, him not loving me, and I wanted him to love me at that very moment. If he had told me he loved me, if he had held me, if he had said something, maybe it would have all been different. But he sat there, sort of staring, saying nothing, and saying so much. I remember him holding me at some point, but his body sort of shook, and I think I terrified him. I think he hated me for telling him these things, for springing this upon him, for expecting an answer. And maybe nothing he said would have mattered, maybe the memory would have always been the same. I was expecting magic, sparks, a happy ending, but I got nothing. We talked for a little while, and when it was all said and done, I got a few words out of him, and that was it. I felt dirty inside. I felt stupid and disgusted with myself. I wanted to take back everything I said, I'm pretty sure I tried to make it seem like it wasn't that big of a deal at some point, but I don't know if he caught on. I was too vulnerable, too trusting, and I wanted to take it back. I wanted it back because I didn't know what we were anymore, and I just gave him so much, poured so much into him and I wanted it all back. I wanted to shove the words back in my mouth and keep them inside of me, hold them so tight and never let go of them again. I told him more than I had ever told anyone in that moment. I told him things I didn't even understand, couldn't even comprehend, I told him those things. And he asked me why, and he tried to understand. Tried not to breakdown, but I didn't see that. I just saw my words spilling out of me, and the trembling girl inside of me running scared. I didn't really give him a chance to process any of it, and then I ran away. I just ran.

That moment was one of the last real ones we had, after that, there was limited contact. Limited conversation. It was a waste of something beautiful, I knew it, but I sold myself a different story, and at that time, I couldn't see clearly enough to see it any different. But I let it out, I put it out there, the stuff I was feeling, the things I didn't understand. The pain, the numbness, the cutting, the everything. It was out there, in the world. I remember him asking me to stop, or if I had stopped, and I told him yes. But the truth was I was licking my lips thinking about the next cut. I had tried to stop, and every time I'd do it, I'd say it would be the last time. I would tell myself I had to stop. I was an addict, this was my drug. *This*, I needed. But I told myself I could stop anytime. Then something would happen, a fight with my parents, a bad grade, an embarrassing moment, and I would get numb, and then the pain would come, and the voices, the screaming, the roaring inside of me would stop. It was satisfied, I would feed the beast and he would quiet down, and it was okay. So when Seth asked me if I stopped I told him yes, I told him yes because I wanted to believe I had, I told him yes because I didn't want him to worry, I told him yes, because inside, I wanted to believe it.

I really wanted to believe it this time.

Chapter 17

the letter.

After much convincing by Clara and Seth, I decided to tell my parents what was going on. I hated that things had progressed so much, to this point. I really believed before this, all those times when my insides were going crazy, when my mind was spinning, when the fire would roar inside of me, I truly believed it would pass. I thought if I just got through this, or that, if I just changed this, if I just satisfied that, I could make it stop. Making the noises, the voices, the screaming, the thoughts, my pain, the void, the aching inside of me, I thought I could fill it, stop it, fix it. At one point I honestly believed it, but the more time passed, the more I came to terms with the fact that this was not normal. This was not something everyone carried, this was not right. I was not right. I couldn't even find the words to describe it, and the friends that urged me to get help couldn't comprehend it either. I'd try to explain these feelings, these moments, but I'd leave out the details that made me seem the most insane, because I wanted to be normal, and I didn't want to give too much away. But at this point, it was too late, there was no turning back, and once I realized I couldn't stop it or hide it anymore, I had to do something. I had been exposed and I had to end it. So I did what anyone in my position would do. Ok, well, I did what someone who was terrified of their parents, terrified of screwing up, terrified of revealing any part of themselves to people who probably didn't give a damn anyway, I did what that person would do. I put it all in a letter. It seemed so normal at the time, it made sense. I didn't realize how absurd it was, to come clean like that. All these thoughts and feelings, all these emotions, I explained them away in my history notebook, and tore them out. After I stuffed them in an envelope, I actually addressed it and put a stamp on it. It probably would have made more sense to just put it in their bedroom, but I knew it would be too easy to back out. To change my mind. After dropping the letter off at the post office, I wanted to undo it so bad, I wanted to take it back, change my mind, and start over. A rush of heat washed all over me and I screamed inside, I wanted a do over, I wanted to pretend, to forget it ever happened. Maybe I could wait for the mail to come like a kid waiting for their report card to hide. I kept picturing Seth's face, kept remembering my lies, my promises. I couldn't go back, so I just waited. I waited for the confrontation.

*Lily sitting on the floor in her bedroom. Her petite frame is propped up against her bed as she sits surrounded by textbooks and notes. Her dad taps on the bedroom door that is already ajar. Lily looks up from her notebook and meets her father's eyes.*

*"Busy?" he questions.*

*Lily shrugs as he walks into the room. She looks back down at her school work.*

*"So, I got your letter."*

*Lily doesn't say a word. She picks up a pen and doodles on her notes.*

*"Are you okay? Was that for real?"*

*"What do you mean?" Lily questions as she looks up at her father.*

*"Are you being serious, the things you said? Do you really feel those things?"*

*"Why would I say it if I didn't?" Lily says with an air of frustration.*

*Her dad sits down beside her and stares at her. She doesn't move, she just sits, staring anywhere but at him.*

*"Is it something I did? Is there something I can do?"*

*"This isn't about you," Lily scoffs and shakes her head.*

Dad couldn't believe I wanted to be dead, that the pain was so extreme I wanted to be gone. Maybe I didn't say it in so many words, but I knew I needed help, because I knew I couldn't do this anymore. He blamed himself for not being around enough, blamed himself for being busy, for not noticing. He made it about him, and I just vanished beneath it. Even my sadness, my pain, my insanity, even that I couldn't have. I was invisible again, under this veil of denial, under this mask of emotion, I didn't care anymore. I couldn't, I shut it off. Strike one.

I was dreading the conversation with my mom. I didn't know how much more of this I could take.

*Lily walks into her room to find her mom changing the sheets on Zoe's bed. She is distracted, tucking in each corner until it looks perfect. Lily enters the room quietly and opens her closet door. Her mom looks up at her and stares at the back of her head for a few moments.*

*"You know the stuff you are feeling Lily, it's normal."*

*Lily doesn't turn around, doesn't look up, doesn't move. Her face is hot, her hands tight.*

*"It's just teenage problems, everyone goes through that," she finishes.*

Numb. I went numb. I wanted to scream, wanted to cry, but I didn't remember how. If this was truly normal, if what I was feeling, if that was something everyone went through, I couldn't comprehend how people went around looking so happy. How people functioned, because I was falling apart fast and this didn't feel very normal. Numb. I wanted to cut so badly, and I did. After our "heart to heart," I went to the bathroom and released the anger, the frustration, and the sadness, all of it, released. But it lacked the same joy it once had, the joy of silence, the quiet stillness it once offered had vanished. Now, now I just felt dirty. I felt like I was cheating on someone, I felt disgusted. I couldn't figure out why at the time, but looking back it was Seth. I told him I stopped, that it was over, that I would never do it again. I was disgusted with myself, no one could ever love me this way. I was becoming the monster. The thing inside of me was taking over, I didn't even recognize myself anymore. I was a shadow of what I once was, I was nothing.

# Chapter 18

## doctors.

Somehow I came to an agreement with my parents about getting help. Dad was somewhere for work and mom didn't really get it, but she took me. I felt like I was wasting her time, and she wasn't really afraid of saying that. I remember going to the doctor for the first time, some little house turned into an office building, turned into a shrink's office, turned into my nightmare. My mom and I went to the office with my little sister in tow. I tried to imagine what she thought was going on. Some random doctor's office, some random day. Her sitting there playing with toys in some childrens' area, while I was in a room, losing my mind.

*Lily and her mom sit on opposite ends of a sofa in a small office. There are books on shelves and certificates in frames. It is quiet. A man in his late thirties sits in a chair in front of them. He has long dark hair and glasses. He looks more like a professor than a doctor in his corduroy blazer.*

*"So Jenny, let's talk about Lily. What brought you in today?" the doctor stares at Jenny as he speaks.*

*"She asked for help," Jenny says with an air of skepticism.*

*The doctor jots a few things down on a notepad and looks over at Lily who is staring at the ground.*

*"Well Lily, what made you ask to come here today?"*

*Lily shrugs at the question and continues to look down.*

*"Jenny, have you noticed any problems with your daughter? Does she seem depressed?"*

*"She says she is depressed, but I haven't noticed anything. She seems quiet sometimes, but she makes good grades and has friends," Jenny explains.*

*Lily closes her eyes.*

*"Well Lily why don't you and I talk for a little while and then after that I will speak with your mom again."*

*"Sure," Lily says sarcastically as she watches her mom get up and leave the room.*

There was so much I kept hidden away, so much I forced inside. So much I could never say. What did my mom think about all those moments, all those memories I had, and all the impulsive behavior? Too busy to notice? Did it ever happen? Was I even there, in that room? I didn't know what was real anymore. But she was right, I didn't advertise my sadness. I didn't walk around with a big sign on me reading: I am miserable, I am depressed, I am in pain, my insides are eating me alive, I am losing my mind, I cut myself, I don't want to wake up in the morning, I am numb. Was I supposed to do that? Maybe I was supposed to wear it all on my sleeve and expose that, but I couldn't. Maybe I couldn't blame her for missing it, for missing my misery. I guess that meant I did my job, forcing it inside, doing everything I could to keep my sanity, to please the monster, to keep it quiet. I had succeeded for so long, I had her fooled. She didn't get this, she didn't get me. I was wasting her time, her baby, my sister, playing with Legos in the other room, she was doomed, because this lady here, this lady next to me in this room, she didn't get it. No one did. I was battling against myself and I was running out of room to breathe.

*After her mom left, Lily sits up a little straighter. The room is cold. The couch Lily sits on is placed in front of a large single pane window. Outside of this room, dark clouds cover the sky and winter chills the air. She wraps her arms around her body as she watches the doctor scribble on his notepad.*

"So what is a normal day like for you Lily?" *he looks up at her.*

"I don't know, what do you mean?"

"What do you do, what is your routine," *he continues.*

"I don't know, I go to school, go home, do homework, hang out with friends."

"Do you have any hobbies?"

*Lily shrugs.*

"Well maybe you should think about getting a hobby. Have you thought about that?"

*Lily just stares at him.*

"Why don't we talk about your family, what are they like, how do you get along with them?"

"I guess okay, I don't know," *Lily sighs deeply.*

"Well what is troubling you today, what made you want to come see me," *he pries.*

*Lily finds a spot on the wall behind the doctor and stares at it.*

"I just don't feel right, I feel depressed, and I just don't know what to do I guess."

*The doctor nods like he has just made some huge breakthrough. Lily wants to scream, or cry, her hands tightening into a fist. She takes a deep breath and sucks the feelings inside for safekeeping.*

"Well, Lily, I know girls your age can feel depressed sometimes. I can see you a few more times and we can get to the bottom of this. How does that sound?"

"Great," *she smirks.*

79

*"Well before I see you again I'd really like you to think about a hobby, maybe video games or something, something fun you can enjoy."*

*She walks past him and out of the room. He sits back down and smiles to himself, truly believing he has saved one more life.*

I felt like an infant. I was a real person with real emotions, but in that office, in that room, I just stiffened up, kept my mouth closed tight. It felt useless. Maybe my mom fooled him already. He believed her. He believed what she said, believed I was okay because she didn't see any difference in me, any changes. Since there were no signs, since I was burying my emotions, I was wasting his time. I hated the feeling of being a burden. He thought whatever it was I was feeling would pass. I wanted so badly for the hell to pass, but I was getting tired of pretending. I wasn't about to get a miracle.

I wasn't very good with doctors. These people, these doctor, you should tell them the truth. What you are doing, what you are feeling, they should know, they could do something, maybe help, maybe anything. But I stopped trusting people, and this guy, well, he was a douche bag and there was no way in hell I could trust him. I could just see him reporting to my mom afterward. Discussing our session and agreeing that I was fine. That everything seemed fine. Telling her he'd see me a few more times, but assuring her it was okay, I was okay, it was just teenage problems. I wanted to vomit. I was sick of this, I was sick.

I met with this doctor a few times, but it didn't get very far. My mom threw a mini fit every time we'd go, the money, the time, not knowing what was she supposed to do, was I fixed yet? And it just got worse. The conversations were so much worse. I would sit there, barely saying a word, I could feel the doctor judging me.

*Lily sits in the corner of the overstuffed sofa. The doctor has a chair pulled up in front of her. Her legs are drawn into her chest. Her eyes are distant, somewhere else, not in the room with him. He stares at her from time to time, but mostly he is taking notes.*

*"I don't think you are depressed Lily," he says, breaking the silence. "I don't think you need to be medicated."*

*She looks at him, not saying anything, just staring.*

*"I think what you are going through will pass, and I really think you will be okay."*

*"So you think this is normal?" she questions.*

*"I think you are overwhelmed and if you practice good habits you can move past this."*

*"Do you think it's normal that I cut myself," she was getting defensive.*

*"Lily, that really isn't good for you to do. You know you could get an infection from that," he explains.*

*Her eyes widen. Her lips tensed on her face and she stares straight through him.*

*"You aren't suicidal are you?"*

*Lily shakes her head.*

*"Cutting isn't a good way to take out your frustrations, this all goes back to the hobby conversation we have been having," he urges.*

*"Okay," she mutters, almost inaudible.*

*"You can come back in a few weeks and we can keep working on this, but after our few meetings I feel comfortable saying you aren't depressed."*

*Lily walks past him, out of the room, down the hall, past the receptionist.*

*"Honey, do you need to make an appointment?" the woman's voice trails down the hall and follows Lily out of the front door.*

*She lets it slam behind her.*

What a waste, what a waste of time. And then I made the decision - if he said I was okay, if he said nothing was wrong, if he said this was all normal, then I guess he was right. I mean after all, he went to school for this stuff. I was just the one living it, but he knew better. So I stopped going. I told my mom I didn't want to see him anymore and we never really brought it up again. As far as my parents were concerned I was healed. I didn't really say anything, I just avoided it all. But if this was what better felt like, I would have rather died. The hell was just starting.

# Chapter 19

## preoccupied.

I had been single for a little while at this point. It seemed like forever, mainly because I was so distracted in a relationship, the time moved so slowly when I was out of one. The strange pseudo-whatever with Seth didn't really count, because I was denying myself from thinking about it, I was hating him for the way he took my confession, and I was punishing myself by avoiding him. In my mind it was probably a lot more overstated and dramatic, because when it came down to it, I think he still thought we could have something, we still had a chance. I hated myself for not trying, for not just giving it a chance, but I told myself there was no way. I loved him too much to ruin him, to ruin us. But it was so selfish, because I was already ruining him, and I was too blind to see it. I convinced myself he probably didn't want to be with me, I explained away his moods, it was just him hating me, he didn't want me, he could never want me. I believed it because I had to, I wish I could take it back, but instead I just moved on. I moved forward. I couldn't stop, couldn't linger, I had to keep moving forward, if I stopped, I might not be able to move again.

I met the next guy through friends at school. Michael was a few grades older, and I was moving my way through high school. So when this new guy, Michael, asked me out on a date, my head spun. He was cute, tall, blonde, had his own car, played guitar in a band, and it was so cool to be asked on a date. No one had ever really taken me on a date before and I felt those stupid butterflies and I loved it. I loved it because I was so sick of these stupid twisted relationships, so sick of everyone wanting me to get help and my parents not getting it, and my insides screaming out again. I was so ready for a change, and this couldn't have come at a better time. So we went on a date, and it was perfect. I was - first date, first date ever, nervous. I was -older guy, car, musician, nervous. I was excited and I sort of felt alive for a few months. I was intoxicated in this dizzying spell of firsts and it felt good to be nervous, and anxious, and smile. It felt good to feel something other than pain and anger. I pushed those feelings down again as much as I could. This was an opportunity to start over, to do this again, to try something new. Maybe I would get it right this time, maybe I really was better. Maybe that idiot doctor fixed me, he told me I was okay, so I was okay. Right?

For a few months I was relatively sane. I stopped the cutting, because I got sick of it, and I had a new drug so I didn't really need it. I loved this new feeling. In my alone moments, the pain would come back. I would close my eyes and picture Michael's face, or imagine some fairytale moments, and it would subside for a little while. It wasn't a permanent fix, but it would do for now, it had to.

So we started dating, and it was really great for a while. I would have these bursts of insanity, but they passed, and it was okay. But the longer we were together, the deeper it got. The more in love he fell. I thought I was in love, that this was love, I just wanted to be happy, and if he loved me I could love him too. I wasn't really sure what love was supposed to feel like. I had this ridiculous twisted love with Seth, but I imagined it wasn't the way it was supposed to be. Seth and I never got a fair chance, because it never went further with us, so I don't know what our relationship love could have been like, where it could have gotten to. Maybe this new thing would be love, maybe this could be love, and maybe love could heal me. The thing was, I needed some sanity, and Michael seemed like a great guy, so I fell into it.

But as time passed, I couldn't fight it anymore. I wasn't happy, I couldn't play the part anymore. I couldn't stuff it, I couldn't fight it. I wanted to but I just couldn't. We started fighting a lot. Mainly it was me, numb, barely responsive, me wanting to cut again, me threatening, quietly threatening to hurt myself. Him going crazy, losing his mind, his anger pouring out from inside. Him bashing in walls on the phone with me, so angry, so scared. And I was afraid of him. What he was capable of doing. But this was love, and I needed someone, I didn't want to be alone. And he was good enough. He was enough.

Michael's life was crazy. Family a mess. His dad had issues, and it was destroying him. He needed me to be his escape, and I needed the same from him, and it was all just too real. This was too real. But we went at it for a while. We had good days and bad days. And then, it started dropping off. I didn't want to be alone so I tolerated. The more I looked at him the more I wanted out. The things that were once cute, the things I loved, enjoyed, cherished, I now hated them, I analyzed him. He wasn't enough, I needed more. But he was good to me, I thought he was good to me, and I didn't want to hurt him. But it all changed, I didn't realize it at first. I was so lost, too confused, and too screwed up to feel for so long that it all just took a while to get to. It took so long to realize the bad, to process it all. He had a hunger I couldn't fill. He had desires, urges I could not satisfy. I didn't want to take things too far, I was worried, scared, I didn't want to do that with anyone, not now, not with this insanity. I was miserable at home, I wanted out, I wanted to get away and I didn't want anything to mess that up. So I would only go so far, I'd only give so much. But Michael wanted to sleep with me and he refused to let me forget that. Nothing I did was enough, because that was what he wanted. Just like I needed these flirtations, these distractions to bridge a sort of sanity, he needed me, needed the intimacy, needed to use me to forget about his weight. He took everything so seriously. Every word. Every idea. Every mention of intimacy. He held onto those things and used them against me. My flirtations, my promises, he needed more, always expected more. And I gave him what I could to get him off my back. I gave as much as I could without giving everything away. Without giving myself away. I was too comfortable in the relationship, and we'd been together too long, so I tolerated his advances. I tolerated the guilt he hung over me when I let him down. I tolerated the talking down, the yelling, the anger, the grabbing. The comfort ran so deep, so much time already invested in this guy, this guy who barely knew me at all. He knew bits of my insanity, he seemed to love me anyway, so it was easy enough to stay with him, because I could keep it at a distance. So I did what I could, gave what I could, and his hunger just intensified.

I remember when I realized there was a problem. Michael was over at my parent's house, hanging out. It was that night I found out a friend of mine passed away. We went to different schools, and we weren't the best of friends, but he was a friend, and we spent time together, and he was gone. I had never lost someone before that wasn't family, grandparents, great grandparents, I'd never lost a friend before. I was so confused. Upset. Disoriented. And this guy, this boyfriend, Michael, he wanted to mess around. I just found out my friend was dead, and he wanted to fool around with me. It made me sick to my stomach. When I resisted, he got upset, like so many other times when I didn't follow through the way he wanted and it would ruin his mood, he was angry, upset, disappointed, cold, hurtful. I didn't know how much more I could take. And the crazy thing is, even just a year before, if I had been dealing with this, this relationship, I would have walked away so fast, I would have run. But I was empty, numb, disconnected. I was losing it and I didn't have the energy to fight this fight. I knew I needed a change, but I was terrified of being alone. It was ridiculous. To stay with him, but I didn't even think about it, I just tolerated it. I knew he had to deal with a lot of crap from me, a lot of ups and downs, a lot of threats, a lot of hurt, so I tolerated him, his moods. His urges, his desires, the belittling comments, his everything. I put up with it, my guilt kept me there, with him. It wasn't until I vented to a friend one night that I heard it all come out of my mouth, that I realized how wrong this way. How crazy I was for staying, for putting up with it, for not running. It's funny how outside perspective can change so much. Once I said the words I couldn't go back. I couldn't face him, I couldn't look at him. I needed out, I needed out fast. This was not right. This was hell, and I was falling apart.

I went to his place one Saturday afternoon, I knew going in that I was going to end things. I knew I had to. But this was a good day with him. This was a sweet day. Maybe he could sense my sadness, my anxiety, my hesitations. No matter how bad it was when I looked it right in the face, it didn't change the fact that we had invested a year together. He knew so much of me, so many memories, moments, it wasn't all bad. It wasn't all bad and I was there trying to remember the good. Trying to hold on a little more. Second guessing ending it, trying to convince myself to try a little more. To keep it going a little longer. To give him another shot. Because the good times, they were good. And there was a time when he was so beautiful to me, when seeing him gave me butterflies, when I wanted to see him, I couldn't get enough. I held so tightly to those times and we sat there at his house preoccupying ourselves. The comfort of staying was so powerful in me. If I could just get past all the crap I could do this, I could stay and this could be good. But it was too late. It was too late because I had shattered the image. I had realized the face of his anger, his breakdowns, I had put a name to it and now it was all I could see.

It ended badly, both of us crying. Him not understanding after all this time, after a normal afternoon, how I could be leaving him. How I could be ending this now. I didn't know what to say. All my arguments vanished and I couldn't think straight anymore. I couldn't stop crying, losing him hurt, and it felt good to feel something. I chose to leave, but it still hurt, and we cried together, and I apologized a million times. But it didn't matter because I wasn't going to take it back. I was not going to change my mind. I wanted out. The thing I forgot about leaving a relationship was how quickly the pain comes rushing back. I had gotten so good at preoccupying myself for a year now, that I forgot how hard the fall was when I was alone. And I fell.

# Chapter 20

## the in between.

Nothing to occupy my mind. Nothing to think about. All I could do was focus my energy on stuffing the emotions back down. I could do this on my own. I knew I had to stay out of a relationship. I needed to master this, I needed to figure out how to tackle the chaos inside of me, I couldn't take it anymore. I couldn't hide it, I felt exposed. I felt naked, empty, and numb. I wanted to scream because everything was so loud inside of me, but I stayed silent, because I was exhausted. The relationship with Michael drained me and I wanted to just do it on my own. No more distractions, I had to figure this out. Had to fix this.

I tried to spend more time with friends. We'd go to shows, go see music, dance, laugh. It was good. I felt ok. I had some good days mixed in with a lot of bad days, but I was looking for something new.

*Lily stands, surrounded by four other girls in the front row of a small club. It's dark inside and there is a band playing on stage. The room is packed with bodies. Lily sways side to side in a pair of tight ripped-up jeans and a midriff baring top. The girls are laughing and dancing to the music. Lily is hyper-aware of her surroundings. Repeatedly glancing around the room as she dances around with her friends. Despite the smiles there is a little uneasiness in the moment.*

I poured a lot of time into friendships, I had burned so many bridges before, I had to put a lot of work into re-building something that would last. It seemed impossible, because I was so sick of being open, so sick of exposing any part of myself. I wanted to go back to the times before anyone ever knew what was going on. Before I admitted something was wrong. I still tried to pretend I was okay, and maybe I was, who knows? But the things I felt, they didn't feel okay. This clawing inside, burning, suffocating, choking me, devouring me, I hated this, this was hell. I wanted the simplicity of a childhood. But even that, even those thoughts weren't pure. They weren't clean. They were tarnished by this thing inside of me screaming to get out. I had become half human, half monster. It was getting worse everyday, but I fought it. I denied it and I stuffed it. But there was no telling who you would get, on any given day. One day I was dancing in the rain with my best friends, and the next I was rolling around on the ground trying to shake the pain out. It was ridiculous, but I had tried everything else I could think of. I needed out, I needed this to stop. Push it down, hide it, bury it. Stop it. Fight it. I had the power.

With all the free time I had being single, I preoccupied myself with little crushes. I figured if I could just get those butterflies back, it would be better than nothing. That would be better, surely it would be better than this. So I scoured the school to find someone. I didn't want a relationship, I just wanted glances in the hall, someone to look for in a crowd of people, someone I never had to talk to, something new. Anything. This didn't go as easy as I had planned. Everything just sort of fizzled out before I could really get started. Everything was escalating in my mental state, it was harder and harder to focus, and I needed a better distraction. That's when I discovered drugs.

## Chapter 21

## and away we go.

I wasn't a stranger to these urges and desires. I had been curious about drugs, fascinated by all of it for so long now it made perfect sense to take the next step. When I was younger, rifling through my parent's medicine cabinet, I didn't understand any of it, but I liked the taste of Robitussin and Triametic, so I explored the curiosity. As I got older, it was the cigarettes. Followed by the mixing of various liquors from Clara's alcoholic mother's stash. I had even smoked pot a few times, but it was never easy to acquire, and no matter how loud the monster roared, I was still terrified of my parents, of messing up, so that kept me at a distance for a long time.

My groups of friends intermixed, and pretty soon it got a lot easier to use. I was a cute girl, which meant most guys would smoke you out and I didn't have to worry about keeping anything at home. I could use caution, and I would be safe. If I just focused on school, kept my grades up, I would be fine. So that's what I did. And when I would breathe in the smoke, it was heaven, totally numb inside, dull, and slow moving. And I felt nothing. All the crap inside, all the fighting with myself, the noises, they all shut off and I could just sit there and feel nothing. It was perfect.

*Lily sits cross-legged on the floor in a small bedroom. The blinds are drawn and it's dark and musty inside. A couple guys are standing around the room while a few more are sitting in a circle with Lily. They are passing a pipe around, lighting and inhaling the smoke before passing it off. Lily is quiet, participating and observing at the same time. The room erupts in laughter and Lily smiles as she closes her eyes and breathes smoke into her lungs.*

I'd still try my old tricks, but whenever anyone mentioned smoking, I was there. I used as much as I could without having to pay. I tried carefully not to overdo it, so no one felt taken advantage of, but I was using the hell out of them. I tried to care, but I couldn't. I needed this. This was my go-to, my fix, my new temporary solution. I didn't know how long this one would last, but it was a little more effective than the other stuff so I dove in head first, and it felt good to fall.

The every now and then increased. It went from weekend parties, from once or twice a month and pretty soon it was every other day, every few days, as often as I could. Then it was everyday after school. But I kept up a front. I was careful, cautious. I didn't want to lose this, something that finally made things okay. The only problem was, when I wasn't high, I was low, really low. I *was on my knees crawling,* low. I was *lost in myself* low, I was dazed, I was numb. Not the same numb I'd get when I was high, the void of emotion numb, the numb I was always used to, the one that was forced out from my lack of dealing with anything. I had shut off my external feelings. Even the relationships lost feeling toward the end, because I had pushed the feelings, the pain, and the misery down so long, I had to fake the smiles. The laughs, they were all forced. And this didn't change when I wasn't using. It only intensified, probably because now I had an alternative. I had a way to push this stuff away, and even if it was just for a moment, it was better than walking around a zombie half the time. But this was a new zombie. I just didn't see that then.

This was a start of something more. I was getting all my close friends involved. I wanted them to take the plunge with me, to experiment with me. I needed some sort of security, I needed people I could trust to go through this with me. And we could experiment, we could immerse ourselves in this. From my perspective, this was okay, this was normal, and this was safe. I was smart, I didn't want to do anything stupid, anything that would get me in trouble. I had big plans. I was going to move away from this small town and I was going to be something. I was going to create, change the world. And I didn't want to get off track. I became more and more cautious as time went on. What used to be these major impulses, the stealing, the rage, the vandalism, these major bursts, all of this was dulled now. I was a slug, I was subdued. I was nothing. I was watchful. I wanted more but I plotted it, calculated the risks. But I couldn't fight it, the impulses were more subtle, but they were still there, they had consumed me completely and I couldn't even see clearly. I should have been found out, I should have been exposed, but I kept my front. I blended in, invisible. Slipping through the cracks.

In the midst of my growing drug use, I got so bored with being alone. I wanted more, I needed something else to occupy my time. It seemed like nothing was ever enough. But I didn't want to look, didn't want to seek it out. There was no one at school that really interested me. I had already burned so many bridges, and I didn't want to see someone every day. I didn't want to deal with an everyday relationship, I needed space. I didn't expect to find it, but it found me.

# Chapter 22

## *obsession.*

He was older, out of high school, a friend of a friend. He was a singer in a band, he was boyish cute, and he was unexpected. He was the last thing I needed. He was Nathan.

We met at one of his shows. I watched him on stage and he was cute, the kind of cute any girl sees when a guy is behind a guitar. He was that kind of cute, but at that moment for me, he was perfect. He was fragile, broken, he was dark, he was interested. I played stupid games with him at first. Stupid flirtation, giving him an open door and acting surprised when he came in. I set him up because I wanted to feel special. I didn't think it would go anywhere, him older, me a fraud. He seemed to like me though, and we started talking more, and it all just clicked.

> *Lily sits alone on the curb in front of a crowded club. Teenagers and young adults congregate on the sidewalk and adjacent street. Lily is looking down at her cell phone as two guys walk over to her. One of them is wearing a white t-shirt and jeans, he has light brown hair and a crooked smile. The other guy is taller with dyed black hair and a thrift store t-shirt. They stand above her until she looks up.*
>
> *"Hey, did the show bore you?" the one in the white shirt asks.*
>
> *"I got a phone call," Lily shrugs.*

*"Ah, got it, this is Nathan, have you met before?" the guy in the white shirt asks.*

*Lily puts her phone down and glances up at Nathan.*

*"Nope," Lily responds.*

*Nathan gives her a wave and she looks back over at the white t-shirt guy.*

*"So when are you gonna make me my mix CD, no more excuses," she smiles.*

*The guy in the white t-shirt plops down on the ground in front of Lily. Nathan stands over them, observing intently.*

Things moved pretty quickly, we went from pseudo-friends, to boyfriend/girlfriend in a matter of days. We had a date to see my favorite band play, which sort of ignited the relationship to begin with. He offered to join me and I was nervous, awkward. Dating an older guy, someone I had some space from, it seemed so perfect, and I didn't want to screw it up. I didn't want to act stupid. I loved the idea of the older guy, and me, stupid screwed up me, felt alive. He poured himself into me. Won me over with songs, with attention. He fooled me, I fell for it.

*Lily and Nathan are standing in line at a Ticketmaster in a small record store. There are a few people in front of them. She is fidgety, swaying from side to side and playing with a rubberband. He is much taller, looking down on her, half smiling with each move she makes.*

*"So, thanks for coming with me," Lily smiles.*

*Nathan puts a hand gently on her wrist, and looks deeply into her eyes. She turns away from him and walks forward as they move up closer in line. He keeps an eye on her, smiling as she pulls away.*

*"I think I should write a song for you," he decides.*

*"You don't have to do that," Lily looks up at him and laughs.*

*He touches her softly, "Well, I'm going to anyway."*
*Her cheeks blush softly and she shrugs, "Ok."*

The more I got to know him, the more I realized how screwed up he really was. He was completely miserable, helpless. He was a mess, and it pulled me in. Finally here was someone who understood everything I felt. I tried to hide my crap so I could help him through his. I didn't want to expose my insanity, for fear that it would cloud what we had. If we combined our pain, it would be disastrous. I wasn't ready for an ending, but I wasn't ready for him either. He was sickly, depressed, manic, impulsive, down, down, and deep down, screwed up. It was magical. I followed him down into his pits, feeling my pain through him. He wasn't afraid to expose himself, it was a part of his art, his music, and I admired his vulnerability. It just wasn't for me, I was impressed. But pretty soon, it pulled at me. His drama, his depression, his stuff, it just piled up, and everything I was pushing down, it just boiled to the surface. It was spilling over into everything, his depression was feeding mine, I waned to push the feelings back down but I absolutely could not. Why did he get to be the one loved and taken care of, why did he get all of my attention, why did he get to be catered to. I needed him, I needed him to take care of me, but he wouldn't. He was incapable of doing anything for anyone else. He expected people to love him, to care for him, to do whatever he asked. I hated it, I was envious of it, but I still did it, I did it because as miserable as I was with him, at least I wasn't alone. He was okay when we first met, he was calm, he was captivating, pulled me in. Now here I was stuck, it was twisted.

I started to get angry, difficult, impossible. My moods were escalating. My drama increased. Pretty soon there wasn't anywhere to stuff it. I had used all my energy taking care of him, I didn't have the strength to bury my misery. And it ended. We ended. He couldn't take it anymore. He needed someone that could care for him, and I was a mess.

*Lily and Nathan sit on the hood of his car in a parking lot. She stares at the ground as he talks. They aren't touching, aren't connecting.*

*"Lily, I just can't do this anymore, I don't know, I just can't."*

*Lily bites her lip hard, not looking up at him. She keeps her head down and pulls at her fingers.*

*"Are you listening?"*

*"Ya," she shrugs.*

*"Well?"*

*"If that's what you want. I don't understand. If there's something I'm doing. I can change. I can be better. I know we have been fighting. It seems so dumb, cause I know we get along so well. I understand you," Lily argues.*

*"I know all of this, I just need to move on, ok?"*

*Lily gets up off the car, doesn't even make eye contact and walks away.*

*"Ok, I have to go."*

*She climbs into her car, turns the radio up loud, rolls her windows down, and speeds off. She looks in her rearview mirror as the parking lot fades behind her and starts sobbing.*

I was a complete mess, and I hated him for ending things. It drove me crazy because for the first time someone walked away from me. Someone couldn't handle me, couldn't love me enough to be with me. It killed me inside. I was a wreck I was so disoriented. With all the pain I had put guys through over the past few years, I had never felt this way before. I didn't even love him, but I loved his misery, I loved his pain so much because it validated everything I felt inside. But I hung on, I couldn't let it go. I couldn't get over it. It consumed my thoughts. What could I have done to fix it, could I have changed it? Made it better, made him stay. Could I win him back, could I re-do what went wrong and try again. It was a drug, he was my drug and I needed him back.

But no, it couldn't be that easy. So I wrapped myself back up in the real thing, more drugs, more distractions. Numb me, make it stop, stop these feelings, these emotions.

*Lily sits alone in her car at a stop sign with the music turned loud. The sky is covered in oranges and pinks and she sits with a joint burning between her fingers. There is a photo of Nathan and her on the passenger seat. As she drives down a back road she pulls the joint up to her lips and inhales the smoke deep into her lungs. As she exhales she turns the music up louder and drives down a long winding road, alone.*

I needed my cover back, I needed to hide again, I needed to disappear again. I needed to be single again, I needed it bad, I needed to get over him, and heal myself. He ruined me, he ruined me because he exposed me to myself. I was a junkie. Not drugs, even though they began to occupy so much of my life, but I was a junkie for him, for the pain I felt, for the misery that consumed me when I was with him. I hated him for letting me go, but I needed more. I needed it even though it was bad, he was bad for me, he was a disaster. I was foaming at the mouth, I was shaking, I hated him. I hated him for getting to me, and I hated myself for allowing him to get that deep. I was used to running away before I got in too deep. Even the love I had felt before for Seth, the intense emotions I'd feel when I saw him, they ignited me, but I ran from them. I didn't want to be vulnerable. I needed my shield up. And this jerk tore it down. I was broken.

*Chapter 23*

*the pieces.*

I covered myself in a cloud of smoke. So many things I had put behind me, I stopped cutting, I avoided relationships, I stopped feeling, I was in a transformation process. I was stoned, and moving forward. I was pulling myself back together slowly, very slowly. But there was progress. This process mostly consisted of a lot of drugs, I tried everything I could. Pot, pills, alcohol, nitrous. I tasted as much as I could, always slightly cautious, always remembering the safer I was, the easier it would be to get out of this stupid town and get the hell away from everything. I wanted to start over, start fresh. I wanted to spit on everything I had, I was losing my mind. I was consumed. I was impossible to be around. My moods escalating, one moment I was okay, laughing and I next I was a mess. I was mascara running, skin peeling, screwed up. It was hard to keep up with the changes. More drugs, more escape, more anything. I couldn't take it anymore. I needed help, again. Self medicating, lying to myself, make believe, it wasn't as bad as it seemed. No, it was worse. I was falling apart, collapsing. I was hearing noises, voices, it was quiet, and it was so loud. The roaring inside, the whispers, the static. It was consuming everything, I tried to scream but nothing came out.

*Dad, I need help.* I had to tell him, I couldn't tell her, couldn't tell my mom. She didn't get it, never got it, and could never get it. Nothing was good enough, it was too much, it was her way, always right never wrong, always in control. I hated the image of her in my head, her face after she read my letter, that seemed like a lifetime ago. I hated her response, I hated her not believing. She was armored, impossible to break through. And my monster, my pain, my life, it was crumbling. So I told him, went to my dad and begged for help. I told him I saw an idiot doctor before, I told him things were bad, worse than they were before. I told him I needed help, I couldn't do it alone anymore. I caved. The stupid beast in me screaming at me for spilling the secret, for exposing myself, it was angry with me. It wanted to take over, didn't want to be fixed. It wanted to live, wanted to run, wanted to do anything and everything, and I was screwing everything up. I was turning him in. I was releasing myself. That's what I believed, but it's never quite that simple.

So dad took me to a doctor across town, and gave her the run down on all of this. On me. Some sob story, something about not loving me enough, not being there enough, not helping enough. He took all the blame, took my pain away from me, he took the credit. But at that moment I didn't really care, because she was going to be my salvation. This woman, she would fix me.

## Chapter 24

## the room.

I sat there with her, with the doctor, alone in a small room. Self-help books lining the shelves of her bookcase. Medical journals, information. Certificates on her wall. She was young, she was peaceful, she was an angel. I didn't know what to tell her. After all the fighting to get here, all the chaos, I was there, and I was silent. I didn't have words for her. I didn't know how to explain it. I was hard pressed to find someone who could actually comprehend the description, and I was just blank, in the room, silent.

I didn't want to expose myself. I wasn't ready to be honest. We talked about my family, about my anger towards them, about the screaming in the house, about the chaos, the nonsense. I gave her a paperback summary of the past few years. I left out a lot of the gritty details. I said no to the drug use questions, I was such a fraud. I wasn't ready to let go. I didn't want to know her diagnosis, I didn't want to hear her, to hear it. I was vague, I stalled, and worded and reworded. It was awkward. This was my "Good Will Hunting" and she wanted to save me.

This became my routine. I started to see her once a month. It was as much as I could do at the time. Mainly because my mom would make comments under her breath about a waste of time, about money, about whatever her twisted head could complain about. I tried to ignore it, stop letting it get to me. But it was impossible. These once a month meetings were my salvation. They were exactly what I needed. During this time everything was changing. It was all getting complicated outside of that room, but that place, it was as close to safe as I was going to get.

I released the gag order and told her more and more, poured my heart out as much as I could, but I still held back, I still held on. I felt naked, and I was miserable. I wanted to cry, wanted to feel with her, but I couldn't. I was strong, I was tough, I hid my tears, and I hid the deeper pains, those things, I stuffed them away. No, I wasn't ready for that. And we moved forward despite the money woes. She wanted to help me, she cared more than she should have. She reworked her pay scale so I could see her on the cheap, she wanted to save me. And I was game.

## Chapter 25

## hung up.

As time passed, I sort of convinced myself I had moved on emotionally from Nathan, that stupid boy who broke me. I was distracted. I was busy with fixing myself, *sort of.* And screwing myself up, *definitely.* Simultaneously. What a mess. I fooled everyone. A friend started dating Nathan and it barely fazed me. Sure, why would I care, our relationship was short lived and I had moved on. The ridiculous thing was that I hadn't. I tried, and I couldn't. I needed a new distraction, I needed another guy, I needed someone else to fill my time, but the truth is I was so pissed off. I was so angry with the way things had ended, and I clung to it, because it was miserable, and I hungered for that.

I needed a secret. And I found one. And it was magical. While my friend, Melissa started dating Nathan, I grew closer and closer to a good friend, Chris. We had been friends for a while, and I was never interested in him. But he transformed almost overnight and the idea of him was so appealing. The only problem was, he was completely hung up. He was head over heels in love with this girl. This girl, his friend, this girl who would not give him the time of day in terms of a relationship. He was miserable, watching her from the sidelines. Obsessing over her, waiting for her. But she showed no sign of running to him. And he confided in me. Shared his prose, his poetry, his beautiful words he wrote for her. And this thing formed, slowly emerged. I showed him my writing, this stuff I sort of hid away, forgot about. The stuff I scribbled in notebooks. The only way I could really express myself. My misery. I shared it with him. And we fell in lust with each other's words. Two stupid, miserable people, so lost, and so desperate for each other. And it just rose from there. We'd get together, we'd talk. We grew closer, but we kept it under wraps. I don't even know why, but it was some sort of unspoken communication between us. This bond, this beautiful thing developing between us, and it was our secret, our beautiful relationship. We didn't need to tell the world. We didn't need a label, we just needed to feel something, we needed a distraction, we needed this.

Chris would complain about the girl and I would avoid talking about the guy, because I was over it. I told myself I was over it. He knew it was a lie, and it made it easier for him to talk about her. I was sort of jealous, because I knew this could never go far. This couldn't grow beyond what we had, it could only be this and stay this. I knew that, but some days I wanted to believe it could be more. Maybe he could be my new fix, maybe we could be more, but I took what I could. It was better than nothing. It was better than being alone.

He would call me after school, after we finished whatever it was we had to finish. I would meet him at the park, back in the woods. We'd smoke some pot, and make out for a few hours. Then we would walk back to our cars, holding hands, holding on so tight, and wishing this would be enough. Some days when we were brave enough, he'd kiss me at my car. The stars exploding in the dark sky, the cool chill of winter creeping up on us, this was nice. It was far from perfect, but it was nice.

*Lily stands in the woods next to a tall, dirty blonde boy with glasses. He is touching her stomach with his hand and smiling at her.*

*"She's crazy for doing this to you, you know that right?"*
*Chris shrugs, "he's crazy too."*
*Lily looks away, fumbles her hands into themselves and averts her*
*eyes. The sky is growing dark above them, but they are there, not*
*talking, not moving, not noticing the shift in the evening. Chris*
*leans in, pulls Lily closer by her waistband and kisses her gently*
*on the mouth and the weight of her body collapses into his arms.*

There was something exciting about whatever was going on with us, we didn't name it, label it, we just lived in it. When we'd cross paths at school, when we were in groups, when our eyes would meet, it was this little secret shared, and it was so good. We were miserable together, me over analyzing where I went wrong, him pining for her. It was so ridiculous when I would get upset, the way Chris would look at her, the way he'd flirt with her. His desperation, him wanting her more than he could find words for, it ate away at me. It was stupid, but it didn't change the way I felt. I was so worried about losing what we had. I didn't want to go public, I didn't want to take it to the next level, I didn't want more, I just wanted it to stay exactly as it was. He was the lucky one, maybe if he had seen me with Nathan, maybe it would have eaten at him too, but there was no interaction there. So it was just me, me watching him.

But it all changed, it would all get quiet for a moment when our eyes would meet across the room and we'd both smile softly. This was a good secret.

We went on like this for a while. My friends were clueless, and it wasn't until much later I found out how clueless they really were. It was one of those campfire, "how many people have you kissed" girl talks, and his name flew out of my mouth. And after all that time had passed, I exposed it. And it felt sort of amazing knowing we had succeeded, we had kept it between us for so long. This special, private thing we shared. This preoccupation of our minds. Us trying to get the other over some stupid unrequited love. I had never dated before, and I guess that's what it was, but it was so much better than that. Looking back now I see how what we had really moved me forward, pushed me ahead and got my mind out of the funk it was in. I got over what I needed to get over and it was so good for that. And when we were ready to move on, we moved on. It was simple. Mostly simple. Because there was still me, not wanting to let the feeling go, afraid I'd go crazy without a distraction, afraid I would have to confront my demons. I needed more of a distraction, I needed so much more. So we walked away, we let it go.

Some nights I would close my eyes, the nights when it got so loud. Not just in the house, but more in my mind. I would turn my music off, lie in bed, close my eyes and remember some star-crossed nights, I'd remember some quiet moments with Chris. Lips, and arms and it was peaceful. I loved peaceful.

# Chapter 26

## *this might get complicated.*

I started hanging out with friends again, the regular group meant shows, it meant seeing Nathan and Melissa, and hearing the songs he wrote for her. It meant hearing them both whine and complain about how much they hated each other. She wasn't with him enough, he was too emotional. She didn't show up when she said she would, he was always asking for money, for food, for rides. He was a mess, she didn't want to tolerate it. But he thought she was beautiful, and that made him feel good. She liked the idea of the guy in the band and the songs, and all that crap. Who wouldn't? So they stayed together, miserable and we all had to hear about it day in and day out.

I thought at this point it was safe to go back into a friendship with Nathan. The main problem was, we never did have much of a friendship, we had a relationship. And the bad part was, all the things Melissa didn't understand, all the junk she didn't want to deal with, I didn't mind. He called and I was there. It felt good to be friends, to talk again. To get to know each other outside of a dysfunctional relationship. It was really nice for a while, and I felt content with the direction of it. I continued to get my counseling, it increased to twice a month and I felt like I was starting to make some progress. It was very slow progress, but it was better than, I don't know. Maybe it wasn't better.

So the friendship with Nathan continued, and while I was working on myself, my head, my insane twists and knots in my stomach, I was falling. Falling, falling into something. I was pretty sure it was love at the time. I was convinced it was a perfect something on the verge of being more. I called it love, but in retrospect, it was not love. In retrospect it was, desperation, it was need, it was I have no idea. All I know is, it was not love. But at the time, that was the farthest thing from my mind. It started out innocent; we would talk on the phone. Him mostly complaining about her at first, which I guess wasn't much different then the secret thing I just got out of with Chris. I guess I was becoming the girl guys confided in. I was the girl you could unveil your soul to, you could be vulnerable with. How the hell was I that girl? I wish I could do that, just release like that. Did it count if I confessed it all to myself? But the twisted thing is, I couldn't even admit it to myself, I couldn't be honest with even me. It was hopeless. It was all so hopeless.

The phone calls turned into hangouts. He lived close to my doctor, so twice a month after my appointments, I'd drive to his apartment. We would just sit there, watch random shows, and sometimes we'd smoke some pot. It was pretty innocent, innocent except for the part where I was falling. Except for the part when I thought maybe he was too. I fought it, I fought the desires, the questions in my mind, I couldn't even comprehend what I was feeling, and so I denied it. I was over this guy, I had moved on, I had my secret relationship. I had my release, I had the time to move past this. But I hadn't moved past it. I couldn't let go of it now no matter how hard I tried. I knew it was impossible, I knew there was no way we could have anything. He was dating my friend, and no matter how much he complained about it, he showed no sign of ending it so I was stuck, the friend. I was there, all time, when he needed something, at the drop of a hat, I was there. It was twisted. He wasn't mine, but I was with him all the time, more than she was. It was fun, and it was hard. Hard because he was miserable, that had not changed. His ups and downs, his frail body, his zombie walk, his moods, his impossible moods. I was there. I sat there and watched him, I held his hand when he was upset, when he was disappointed. I drove him to get food, I did what I needed, I thought if I could be there for him, I don't know what I thought, I was just there. If it had just stayed that way, if it had just been me avoiding the feelings, me thinking it was more than it was, if it was just me it would have been fine, I could have lived with that. I could have, but slowly everything started to change, slowly everything just transformed.

On the weekends a group of us would spend the night at his hole in the wall apartment. A bunch of my friends, but never her. Never his girlfriend. We'd all pile into one big bed and fall asleep stoned after watching hours of old TV shows. Most nights he would fall asleep next to me, or he'd find his way next to me, somehow. Our bodies would touch gently at night, and I felt guilty for being so close to him, I knew it wasn't right.

> *Lily walks into a messy, poorly lit bedroom. Clothing is scattered around the room and the bed is simply a mattress on the floor. Five or six people are sitting around the room, a mixture of guys and girls. As she walks in her eyes find Nathan lying on the bed, laughing as he watches TV. She diverts her eyes to one of the girls as she walks deeper into the room. As Nathan sees her, he jumps up and greets her. As the night continues they find themselves next to each other on his bed that now holds several other people. Lily slips her body under the covers and falls asleep, with Nathan beside her, never moving. He inhales her scent as he closes his eyes.*

I tried to tell myself it didn't matter because all they did was complain about each other and why should I have to wait, why should I have to wait for them to end it, for him. Why should I have to stop. But the guilt ate away at me, and I know it ate away at him too. The moments were pretty innocent, but we both felt the guilt of them. Then he came clean, and just when I thought I was okay, that I could move on, he pulled the rug out from beneath me.

*It's morning in Nathan's apartment. His room is empty except for his sleeping body in the bed and Lily grabbing her things from the couch. He opens his eyes and looks up at her.*

*"I have to go," Lily explains.*

*Nathan sits up and stares at her for a moment.*

*"We can't do this anymore, It's not right, it isn't fair, we can't."*

*Lily takes a deep breath and nods.*

*"I have to go."*

He said all these things and I died a little inside. I knew he was right, but I wanted so badly to be the one to hurt him. We still hung out. He still called, we still talked all the time. I tried to distract myself. I tried to focus on anything besides him, but it was all the same, he would call, and I would run. He said jump and I did. I was disgusted with myself. I had gotten so far, I had grown, I had changed, and I had fixed this tiny part of myself. Everything else was still a disaster, but this, this I had fixed. I thought, I had it all figured out. It was the misery crawling back inside of me again. The way it had been before when we dated, all of that bubbled back to the surface. I was becoming a zombie, it drove me crazy but I couldn't stop. Always addicted to something, always needing a fix. This time it was everything rolled into one. So many vices, so much crap just there. I wasn't sure if it was him escalating my depression, or if it was just a coincidence. My moods slowed, the ups and downs became downs, and they lingered. They lingered and I waited. I waited for him to change his mind, to admit I wasn't the only one feeling this. The days turned to weeks, turned to months, turned to me, crazy me. Why can't he see me, want me. Everything was crashing down around me. I couldn't live in my skin anymore. At home, it was impossible, it took every ounce I could muster to deal with my mother's nagging, my siblings fighting, my dad's moods, chaos. I felt like I was blending in the background and I didn't have the strength to scream.

Then, one day, I just couldn't take it anymore. I was tired of our back and forth, of me wanting more, of him avoiding. There were these moments still, this flirtation, these lines we'd cross, then we'd draw new ones, and we'd teeter on the edge. I needed answers. I couldn't handle the let's talk about it later, lets just watch TV, smoke some pot, let's just forget about these feelings. I wanted to forget but I couldn't. I would avoid him, I would stop spending time there, I wouldn't answer my phone, but he would still call. He kept calling. The more I avoided the more he advanced. It was what I was waiting for, but it wasn't enough. Finally I called back and went over to see him.

*Lily knocks on Nathan's apartment door. Without much delay he answers, and stands tall before her.*
*"Want to get some lunch?" he asks.*
*"I don't really have money to buy us anything right now."*
*Nathan lets the doors close behind him and he walks Lily toward her car, "Don't worry, I'll buy, I have coupons," he smiles.*
*They sit at a small table at a fast food place. Lily eating a carton of french fries and Nathan a burger. They don't really talk, they talk around things. Eat their food, kill time. Out of nowhere Nathan opens his mouth.*
*"I love you," he says without looking up.*
*Lily's heart stops beating in her chest, then immediately goes at full speed. Struggling to catch her breath she paints her french fry into a blob of ketchup.*
*"I always have loved you, this whole time, even before, I just don't know how to do this. I don't know how to be with you. I know*

*we tried before and it didn't work, but I think we can do this now, I think we can get this right."*

*Lily looks up at him bright eyed, but logical.*

*"Nathan, no we can't. Are you forgetting Melissa? I don't understand where this is coming from."*

*"Don't you agree, don't you love me too? Don't you want this?"*

*"Nathan, that's not the point, the point is you are in a relationship with my friend and it can't work. Maybe she isn't around but you still chose her and you're still in this."*

*"I know, it's complicated."*

*"Well, then uncomplicate it, if you want this so bad, leave her."*

*"It's not that easy. Things are ending, I want to just let it run its course."*

*"It never is with you. Do you love me?"*

*"Yes, I said I do, and I do."*

Everything I had always been waiting for him to say, to feel, he had already been thinking, feeling, and pushing away. He was fighting it as much as I was. It killed me. Mainly because I knew nothing would change, we wouldn't move forward. He would stay with her, in this place, until the life was drained from the relationship and it withered away. And even though it felt over, when they were together, it was different. They were both so different. He begged me to wait for him, to hang out, to give him more time. He almost cried telling me he wanted me, to be with me, he needed me, and loved me. He asked me to wait, and I was stupid, so I said I would. I didn't understand how it would work, how it could happen, how things could change, when things ended with them, how could they start with us. Would it be some secret thing again? And this time it was different. It was different because I was even better friends with Melissa now, then I was before. And our relationship was so short lived before, it didn't seem to matter. But it mattered now, it had to. When I left that day I didn't know how to feel. Should I be happy he finally admitted he loved me, needed me. Or should I be miserable, should I hate him for not just making it work so that we could finally try this. Finally do this the right way. It took so long for us to get to know each other, to understand each other. If we did it this time, if we tried it this time, then maybe it would all be different.

At home, when it got loud, when being alone was so unbearable, when despite all the noise we were all living in silence, it was then that I closed my eyes and heard Nathan again in my head. Asking me to wait, begging me. I let the tears stream from my eyes, finally, what I wanted, just out of my reach, it was terrible. I felt guilty when I saw Melissa at school the next day, my friend. We talked about stupid random things and all I could do was picture him and me lying together in his bed crowded with people, and me, sleeping in his arms. It was distracting. The guilt ate away at me. I sort of sat by for a while, waiting. Trying to distract myself for the time being. Trying to put my mind somewhere else. I could wait, I told myself, I could sit by, I could wait. And I really thought I could.

# Chapter 27

## exactly what I needed.

One of my best friends at the time, Maya, lived out of state. South Carolina. She moved there in middle school and we stayed close, got closer after she was gone. She was one of the few people I could tell everything to, well as close to everything as someone like me could get. It was somehow better, easier being far apart. Didn't have to fight, didn't have to deal with the stupid things most people do. We communicated on the phone, long emails, letters. She knew a lot about what I was dealing with, the stuff about the doctor and the boys, not as much about the darkness, about the demons. I knew her stuff too. It was the perfect friendship, and it only got better. We would see each other a few times a year and it was incredible. Sometimes I'd go down to South Carolina to visit her, I'd spend a week there, and it was always amazing, always so much stuff crammed into such a short amount of time. I remember this one time I went, right in the middle of the back and forth with Nathan, and I needed out. I needed an escape. I so looked forward to the chance to get away from him, from his calls, from the awkwardness, from the waiting.

Maya was working at an independent theatre when I went down there to see her. I loved the lifestyle, the freedom. Her in some small beach town and all the people, so carefree. I wanted so badly to be carefree. I didn't even know what that would look like. I was so far from carefree, it was ridiculous. I was distracted, chaotic, obsessive, compulsive, depressed, impulsive, I was nowhere near carefree. But this trip and the trips to follow, they were my escape, my chance to be a different person, to live a different life for a few days. It was bliss. It was the best distraction. A new set of problems, people, situations, I got to sneak in and sneak back out.

I remember walking into the theatre that first night there and meeting everyone for the first time. This world she lived in. It was so new, the people were great, and it was a complete change of pace. Her two closest friends down there were Amy and Eric. They were excited to meet me and the feeling was mutual. I had heard so much about them and was glad to finally have faces for the names. Eric was shy, sort of cute, but not really my type. Not that it mattered, I was there to escape, not to find a guy, a long distance relationship. So I met everyone and we hung out at the theatre for a while, and everything was fine, almost perfect, until I saw Taylor. He was the theatre manager, olive skin, dark hair, a smirk of a smile. I remember Maya telling me about him, and it really didn't do him justice. He was perfect. Probably way too old for me, but it didn't really matter because I was just watching him. I knew there wouldn't be anything more than that, but it was fun to watch him. To stare at him. He was captivating. I watched him put the films on the projector, watched him sit at his computer in his office doing paperwork, and I tried to keep my cool. Maya's friend, Amy, had a huge crush on him. They all talked about how they just wanted to grab him and randomly kiss him just for the hell of it, and I joined in, how we'd do it, when, where. It was fun to think about these things instead of all the stupid drama I was dealing with back home. It was simple there. I knew it wouldn't last, I knew the feelings of peace would go away after I got back home, so I savored these times.

Our days were spent driving around, smoking, and listening to music. Our nights were spent hanging out at the theatre, or watching a show, drinking, relaxing. We'd sit up late, at the theatre after hours, drinking and watching films on the big screens. We didn't have to think and I didn't have to feel. Maya and I would sit and talk about our guy issues, my drama back home, and her drama there. We would advise each other on the situations, and then waste time, doing nothing. I loved it. But my crazy mind kept going back to the guy, Taylor, her boss, I was fascinated by the idea of him, and I was hoping that he would see me, notice me. I knew it was so impossible, but I knew it would take my mind off all the crap at home. To know there was someone that could fall for me, that someone I thought was way out of my league could, would notice me. It was so stupid how I based these moments, the things around these guys, these stupid guys that I allowed to consume me, but it was all I knew how to do. It was all I had.

The trip was coming to an end, and I was losing my ability to focus. I wanted to stay there, I wasn't ready to go. And I felt empty, I felt like I needed something, I needed to fill the void. How could I go back home, how could I face the situations I had left behind, I was desperate for an escape, desperate to get something to occupy my time, my mind. I kept thinking about Taylor, I wanted to say something. I wanted to do something, knowing I was leaving and not knowing if I would ever even see him again. I just wanted to act on the impulse. I was longing for the impulses I had at one time. I felt so dead inside, and I just wanted to shake it. I wanted someone to want me back. I wanted someone I didn't have to wait for, didn't have to fight for. I wanted someone to fight for me, and even though I didn't see that happening now, it was okay. I could do it, I needed to.

*Lily walks into the Movie Theatre wearing a long tight red skirt and stomach baring top. Maya is behind the snack counter in the middle of the lobby and Lily struts over to her, head held high. Taylor walks thru the lobby to a staircase on the other side of the room. Lily keeps her eyes fixated on Maya behind the counter, ignoring Taylor as he walks past. He glances over at her, his eyes moving along the curves of her body.*

*"So where's Amy?" Lily asks Maya.*

*"Upstairs maybe," Maya shrugs and she fills a tub of popcorn.*

*Lily fiddles with a napkin on the counter and eases away from the concession stand and heads up the staircase. She wanders around upstairs, through the hallway, running her hand along the wall. Her heart racing, her eyes scanning the area. She stops outside of an office and peeks her head in. Amy is sitting in a chair looking through a notebook and Taylor is behind the desk on a computer. She hurries past the door.*

*"Lily!" Amy screams from the office.*

*Lily stops in her tracks, heart thumping. She slowly makes her way to the office and peeks her head in.*

*"Hey, what's up?"*

*Taylor doesn't look away from the computer screen. Lily watches him from the corner of her eye.*

*"Do you want to go out for a smoke?" Amy wonders.*

*"Ok, sure, I guess."*

*Amy gets up from the chair and walks out of the office, Lily lingers there for a moment, trying to catch Taylor's eye, to no avail.*

*Lily and Amy sit on the curb smoking. The air is calm, salty. It's humid and Lily leans back slightly letting the gentle breeze blow across her skin.*

*"So what's up with Taylor tonight, he seems moody."*

*"Yeah, I know, no clue, he has been in a bad mood since I got to work. He's so hot."*

*"Yeah, he is." Lily takes a long drag off her cigarette. "Eric's kinda cute, huh?"*

*Amy perks up.*

*"You like Eric?"*

*Lily shrugs.*

*"I don't know, he's cute, I just need a change. I don't know if he likes me."*

*Amy laughs.*

*"He thinks he's out of your league, besides, I thought you were into Taylor."*

*Lily lies down on the sidewalk and closes her eyes.*

*"I don't know what I want anymore."*

Never realizing the true impulsion was always there, under the surface. It was there in the back and forth, the one guy after another. It was mostly innocent, but I got bored, needed the butterflies, and needed to feel more, always needed to feel. I needed some sort of twisted validation. Some reason for my existence. And it got stuck in my head and I couldn't let it go. So I preyed on Eric. The sweet guy who turned red when I walked into the room. I tried to ignore it, but I knew, I knew if I pushed he would cave. I knew if I asked, if I acted, if I just moved, didn't think, I knew he wouldn't push me away. So I poured it all into him. The stupid flirtation, the feelings, the desires, everything I was feeling for Taylor, this guy I barely knew, but I wanted it, I wanted the excitement of something new, and he gave it back, he fell for it. He was consumed by it. But it was fleeting.

*Lily and Eric sit cozily in the back row of an empty theatre. "The Matrix" is on the big screen. Eric kisses her ear gently as she stares up at the screen. Out of the darkness a soft glow of light appears, a door opens and Taylor walks in. Seeing Lily and Eric snuggling in the dark he shakes his head as he walks toward them. Eric tightens his arm around Lily as Taylor gets closer.*

*"Ok then," Taylor shakes his head.*

*Lily fidgets with her hands. Looking at Taylor from the corner of her eye, nodding a goodbye. Eric puts his hand out to Taylor.*

*"Later buddy," Taylor pauses. "Have fun," he says with hesitation.*

*Lily winces under the weight of Eric's arm. Her eyes follow Taylor as he walks away. Eric kisses her neck gently as her eyes move back to the screen.*

*"I'm so glad you came here," he says in-between kisses.*

*Lily forces a smile across her face.*

*"You're a breath of fresh air."*

*Lily turns to look at him, "What do you mean?"*

*Eric runs his hands along her arms, "Don't know, you're just different, there is no one like you here, you're amazing."*

*"Uh, ok, you're crazy," she laughs. "I should probably go, Maya is waiting," she twists out of his grasp.*

*Standing now Lily leans down and kisses him lightly on the mouth. "Bye Eric."*

*He grabs her hand as she walks away and she shakes him off, forcing a smile until she gets to the door. As she walks from the theatre to the car her face drops more and more. Her arms wrapped around her body, holding herself together.*

Instantly I knew I would be kicking myself later, I knew I would regret messing with him, pretending with him. It wasn't that I didn't like him, wasn't interested. It was that I was leaving and when it came down to it, he wasn't what I wanted. I hated myself for it, but at least I wasn't going home lonely. At least I wasn't just sitting around waiting for someone to notice me. I was going to take control.

# Chapter 28

## *jealousy.*

Back to reality. Not much had changed. Things were okay with my doctor. We were analyzing my symptoms. Everything seemed ever changing and I was so up and down. Sometimes we would just sit in the room, her talking, me staring. Other times I was telling her a million things, unable to stop myself. I felt like a lost cause, but she wanted to fix me. She put me on an anti-depressant hoping that would help stabilize me. I didn't really know if it was working. I felt the same. Nothing really changed. But she wanted to figure it out. My inconsistencies weren't helping. The drugs probably didn't help much either, but I had to do something, and self-medication was all I could think of.

Things were relatively the same. I was going through the motions. Still waiting for Nathan, but growing anxious. I didn't think about it as much as I used to, it felt like moving on, not quite there yet, but it felt close. Summer was coming soon, and that meant Maya would be in town most of the summer, and I was longing for it. Even though I had just been with her, I was already longing for the comfort of our friendship. I knew everything would change with her there, she would watch me in these moments, these interactions and she would be honest with me, she would understand me in those moments and I sort of needed some outside perspective. She was the only one who knew what was going on with Nathan, and I needed her to tell me to get over it or to push forward. This summer was going to be different though. Her new boyfriend Jeremy and her friend Eric, the guy who I shared the moments with a few months back, they were going to come for a visit. It made me anxious. I knew what had happened with us, I knew it probably didn't mean much, to me, I knew there was so much more here that I wanted. I was waiting for someone, but I was sick of waiting. It was awkward, thinking about Eric coming, knowing he expected something, missing me, wanting to know me, thinking I could take him out of his normal, everyday life, and ignite him. But me, I wasn't ready for that, couldn't be that for him.

So Eric and Jeremy came to town and spent a long weekend with us. It was awkward between Eric and me. Awkward because the truth was, I was still hung up on Nathan. I had no right to be, I was stupid and I probably deserved better, but honestly I didn't feel like I even deserved him, I wasn't good enough, never good enough.

Here was this guy, Eric, crazy about me, waiting for me to make a move, to give him the time of day, and I couldn't go there. I felt terrible. I hated myself for pursuing something when I was visiting, I hated myself for making this awkward. But it was too late. He tried to flirt, tried to talk, tried to advance me, but I pushed him way. So cold. I couldn't do lukewarm. I couldn't fake it anymore, I didn't have the energy. I didn't have the heart. I needed to explain it, and eventually I did.

> *Lily and Eric sit on a big couch in a dark room. The TV is on, flashing music videos with the sound down. Lily holds a pillow between their bodies. Eric inches his body as close as possible, but not close enough. She stares off in the distance and his eyes direct their full attention on her.*
> *"Hey," he says softly to break the silence.*
> *"Hey," followed by a deep sigh from Lily.*

*"I'm glad I get to see you again."*
*Lily turns to him, stares at him for a moment before turning away.*
*"Things are complicated here. I don't know what to do. I like you, you are great and I want to get to know you better, but there is drama here."*
*He sits silently, watching her intently.*
*"I want it to be different, I thought it would be, but it just isn't right now. Please don't hate me."*
*Eric shakes his head and touches her arm softly.*
*"I don't hate you, I understand. I can't just expect to come here and everything to be exactly the way I want it."*
*"Are you sure?" she questions.*
*"Well it sucks, but yeah, it's okay."*

After the awkward "break-up" or whatever you want to call it I stumbled upon a miracle. It was so simple, so stupid, but it changed everything. The four of us went to a house party. Most of the people were older, friends of friends, and Nathan, the stupid guy I thought I loved, was there. Everyone hung out, watched movies and relaxed. I let Eric flirt with me, I figured it was harmless and I would flirt back. By this point he already knew I was stuck on someone, he knew there was drama, he knew I wasn't ready, not now. And after that was gone, after it was out in the open it was easier just to be together, to hang out, and not to have to think about it. It was fun, I was carefree, the way I needed it to be.

Later in the evening Maya pulled me aside, this was the moment I was waiting for, but I was having such a good time I almost forgot I needed her to observe, to explain the chaos to me. She was freaking out, she was bright eyed. I didn't understand. I just remember her telling me Nathan was jealous, this stupid guy who kept me waiting, who kept saying he wanted me, couldn't have it, wasn't the right time, this jerk, he was jealous. He wanted me, he knew he couldn't have me, he knew I was moving on. I had told him, but he didn't believe me, and now he was seeing it. I didn't know how to feel, but I just smiled. His girlfriend was there that night, shocking because they were barely together. Maya told me he was clinging to her tightly, being extra affectionate but I didn't even notice. I was just enjoying the company of my friends, and the guilt I felt for leading Eric on, well I was doing everything I could to make it better, to make it up to him. I didn't want him here, to come here and me be all wrapped up in someone else. So I just enjoyed his company and forgot about Nathan, forgot about what I wanted, what I had wanted so badly up to that moment. And I hated that he was there, holding on to his girlfriend, hoping he could get to me like I was getting to him. It was ridiculous. It was disgusting. I loved it. Finally, I had the upper hand.

We hadn't planned on spending the night, but we all sort of fell asleep and stayed there. In the morning Nathan cornered me as I was gathering my things to leave. His girlfriend was asleep in the other room, he heard me wake up and ran down the stairs after me. I could see the jealousy in his eyes, and I hated him for running after me with her in the other room sleeping in his shirt. He told me he wanted to be with me, he needed me. He apologized for taking so long to end things. He asked me if there was something going on with me and the guy from out of town. I told him there had been and I wasn't sure what was happening now. He told me to stop, to be with him. To forget about the other guy. God, this was ridiculous. I had been waiting so long for him to beg for me this way, and all it took was showing up to a party with someone else. If I had known that I would have done it a long time before. But I guess it would have been a lot different. I wasn't really sure what I wanted. But I had the power. I was in control now. It was beautiful.

# Chapter 29

## i want you back.

After the night Nathan confessed he wanted me, I secretly waited to see if he'd make his move, if he would finally end things with Melissa. Somehow I was still shocked when things stayed the same. I had avoided him, I wanted to give him space so he could take care of his stuff, so he could move on, so he could get his head straight. And it gave me time to get my stuff straight as well. We ran into each other one day, somewhere, and his eyes, they longed for me. It was sad. Him stuck in this relationship he was too scared to get out of. Wanting me, needing me, and he couldn't have me. I was right at his fingertips, but his arms weren't long enough. All he had to do was let go, and he was too screwed up for even that. But I was screwed up too, so it didn't really matter. He wanted me, I could see it, and I felt alive. And this little part of me gave up, stopped caring. I got what I wanted and slowly I was moving on. I was moving on because I had to. Part of me still clung to the idea of him, because there was nothing else to divert my attention, but the idea of him was no longer enough. I needed something different. It all just felt pointless.

## Chapter 30

## the boys then.

Even when I was a child, I was already discovering the simplicity of a man's mind. I was also discovering the power of a woman. I was seeing the interactions. I was witnessing these boys, their needs then, so similar to when they grew up. Not fully getting it then, but I connected the dots slowly. Even when I was younger there were the relationships. There was the power these boys would give you. There was this control. This confusion. Not really understanding where it all came from but knowing there was some meaning in it. So often I found I was the girl who wanted the guy she couldn't have. The girl who was wanted but all these guys, none of them good enough. None of them what I wanted. And there was me, not trying, not putting forth much effort. And there was them, running to me. I didn't get it, and in a way I still sort of don't but I remember how it felt to be wanted. To be the center of someone's world, and I knew I liked that. I knew I wanted that. And maybe when things got bad, when it all got worse, there was this comfort in getting that back. In feeling like I was the center of someone's world. So I didn't have to think about how my world was falling apart.

When I was young, very young, I remember these moments. This boy, so into me. Saying he loved me. We had to be seven or eight years old then. And he was so into me. He was wanting to hold my hand, wanting to be near me in whatever way kids want to be near each other then. And it was okay. It was nice to have someone to hang out with. Someone to entertain me. But I doubted it even then. I challenged it. I second guessed everything. The paranoia setting in even then. I didn't want to let go. Didn't want to give of myself. I didn't trust. I was suspicious. The powers of human observation. Me so in tune with everything surrounding me. I kept my guard up, kept my walls from falling down. I felt that then. I did that even then. And in the back of his dad's car on the way to a birthday party, as we sat there holding hands he told me he loved me, I threw it back in his face, because I didn't believe that. I didn't believe him. I told him he didn't love me, that he just loved my hand. And he was speechless, eight years old and speechless. It didn't seem like a big deal to me then, I just didn't trust him. I was always over thinking. Over analyzing even then. It made my head spin.

There were those little boys who showered me with gifts. Gave me rings, yes rings. There were the I loves you's, and then there was me not really understanding it. Not getting why they were so into me. It made me feel strange, awkward. And I don't understand where these weird gaps came. Me and boys. Me feeling not good enough. Me doubting them when they wanted to be with me, when they said they loved me. Because growing up, it was so opposite, it was me fielding them, me pushing them away. Me either loving them or hating them in the way a seven year old would. There was me giving back the rings. Embarrassed by the gifts. It was such a strange time. It was nice being wanted.

But as time passed. As I got older, as all these other elements came into play. As I started doubting. Started questioning. Started hearing things louder. Hearing these whispers. Over thinking. Over feeling. Every moment lying in question. Everything hanging on the edge waiting for me to make my move. As time moved on, it was chaotic. It was the sounds in my head. The rustling in my gut. It was the fears of inadequacy. It was my self image. My self confidence. My self-esteem. Shattered. Shafted. Diminishing. It was the awkward years. It was me slowly beginning to hate myself. It was me giving in to the pain. Giving into that part of myself that wanted to corrupt me. That wanted to destroy me. It was this constant back and forth and it was me barely floating above the surface. It was all these things rolled together. And it was the complexity of one life I lived, this life where I was magnificent. And it was the contrast of me, nothing. Me losing everything. Me becoming all of these things I hated. It was these two lives. These two beings. These two stories merging into one. Seeing which could overpower the other. Testing each other. Seeing who would win the battle. Wasn't sure who to fight for. It was the angel and devil on my shoulder. It was the demon in the pit of my stomach. It was me trying to figure out who the hell I was and not wanting to see the answer. It was these two things living inside of me at the same time. It was the conflict. The confusion. The double talk. It was all of those things, then, and now.

And as I got older, as I continued to exist in the realms of relationships. After I was loved. I was loved and I pushed it away, because I had stopped believing it. I had stopped believing in that. It was then that the devil, that the demons were gaining the upper hand. It was then that the gentleness was pushed deeper and deeper down. And so much of the time when I tried to push the pain away, it was all a mess. This complicated disaster. All of it living inside of me. Not allowing any love to get in. These small cracks in me and I was sealing the surface. I was closed for business. I was lost, and I didn't think I could be rescued.

## Chapter 31

## chemicals.

The doctor decided to try me on a new antidepressant. At this point she had diagnosed me with major depressive disorder, but it didn't all fit. She was still trying to figure me out. So I took my pills and hoped they would fix me. But I still felt the gnawing inside, I still felt my stomach tying itself in knots. I tried to focus, but I couldn't. On the outside I had it together. The grades, the ambition, the dreams. But I would just sit there, scribbling away in my journals, writing, creating, releasing the crap I couldn't explain, some beautiful description of disaster lining the pages of my notebook. These drugs, the ones they prescribed, the ones that were supposed to fix me, nothing worked, and nothing changed. I hated this. This feeling. I wanted to scream. Nothing came out. My mom still nagging about the costs, my dad distracted, siblings, drama. I hated it, I hated being around it. I was invisible in that house. Partially because I made myself invisible. I wanted to slip through the cracks, I wanted to go unnoticed so I could keep things as they were. Some crazy idea of freedom that barely made sense. But at the same time I wanted to be seen. I wanted someone to notice my misery, but in order to function, in order to get out of there I had to succeed. What a confusing place to be in. I was losing my mind, slipping away, trying to be everything to everyone. It was ridiculous. I hated myself. I hated the insanity, I wanted to die. I couldn't take it anymore.

I was hoping we were getting closer to an explanation at the doctor's office, in our meetings. The noises, the shadows I saw, the whispers, the static. I didn't know if it was an extension of something else, or if the main problem was that I couldn't think straight anymore. I wanted the doctor to stop it, I wanted the quiet. My personal life was so dysfunctional. Such a fraud, I was such a phony. Hiding everything I was feeling. Half sane. This was getting ridiculous. When the prescription didn't work I'd just self-medicate some more. All the time, every chance I could. Something had to change.

I wanted to be locked up. Throw away the key. I heard about a program at a local hospital. Some rehabilitation thing. I wanted to be rehabilitated. It sounded like heaven. I was ready to explode. Falling apart inside and still functioning. Still projecting the "I'm okay" image. I wanted to just let go, to allow myself to just feel everything inside without fear of falling apart in front of everyone. I wanted a safe place. Somewhere I could come undone. Once I got the idea in my head I couldn't stop obsessing over it. I just wanted to take off, I wanted to leave, I wanted to release myself. I wanted to stop pretending everything was fine. I thought being locked away was the perfect solution. I thought if I could just get away for a little while, if I could come undone, then I could put the pieces back together. I thought I could be whole again. I didn't remember what whole felt like, and the more I thought about it, the more I thought it maybe never existed. I didn't get my wish, I got reality instead.

# Chapter 32

## a second chance.

Soon enough it was time to go back to South Carolina. I was looking forward to another escape. A lot had changed since my last visit, and so much was still the same. I was convinced this trip would shake me. I felt anxious going back, not knowing how things would be with Eric after the summer visit. The guy I sort of lead on, sort of let go. I was sort of crazy about him for opening Nathan's eyes, but I was pretty sure it would be awkward. Even though we talked it out, I knew it wasn't fixed, it couldn't be that simple.

It smelled so good when I got off the plane. It was the smell of freedom and it came rushing back over me. Everything was perfect, simple, then Maya said his name. Taylor, the guy, the boss, the film guy. Amy and Maya talked about him, discussed him. Amy had this tiny crush on him before, and it was growing. She was pretty sure he was into her and she was so happy, ecstatic, content. And I was happy for her. I was happy for her because this was her town, her place, and I was just a stranger, a visitor passing though. But all that went out the window when I saw him, I saw Taylor and it all came rushing back. He was more beautiful, more perfect than I remembered. An instant rush of guilt washed over me, I hated myself for stopping dead in my tracks when I saw him. I hated myself for allowing my stare to linger. I wanted him and I couldn't help it. This was a mess, I was a mess. Just back in town for a visit and I was already burning bridges.

Somehow Taylor and I ended up alone, and it was this awkward conversation, us catching up, even though we barely exchanged much dialogue the last time I was around. I was flustered, I was captivated. I tried to play it cool, I tried to hide it, I felt stupid. Feeling this way for someone I barely knew. It all seemed so innocent, I was caught up in my imagination, it almost didn't feel real.

*Taylor stands by a projector, switching things on, positioning a reel of film. Lily leans her body in the doorway. Her eyes watch his every move. His hands carefully adjusting the machine, his eyes intently focused. After the film starts, he looks over at Lily who is fixated on him.*

*"Hey there, you're back," Taylor comments.*

*"Yup," she nods.*

*They both stand at opposite ends of the room, her heart racing, his hands twitching slightly in the silence.*

*"Did you just get in," he walks closer to her.*

*"Couple hours ago."*

*Lily doesn't move, doesn't flinch, her body presses hard against the door frame. Taylor gets so close she can feel his breath. Her heart racing, pounding in her chest, so afraid he can hear it.*

*"Do you have a minute?" he questions.*

*Lily turns away from him for the first time since walking into the room and looks behind her toward the stairwell. It was empty.*

*"Sure, what's up?"*

*"What did I do wrong?" he leans in close to her.*

*Lily's eyes narrow, her throat tightening, heat rushing over her.*

*"What do you mean?"*

*"I know I messed up, I just don't know how. I was giving you all the signs, what did I do wrong."*

*Lily is frozen, confused. Her eyes, questioning his.*

*"I just don't understand why you chose him? What did I do wrong?"*

*He is so close to her now, she can't move, even if she wants to.*

*"I'm really confused, are you saying you, I'm just," she stumbles through the words.*

*"I just really liked you, when we met before, I was crazy about you. I thought for a minute you might be interested, but then that night, I saw you with him."*

*"You liked me, then, before?"*

*Taylor laughs, laughs like she's crazy for even questioning him.*

*"Come on, you knew, you had to know," he pushes.*

*"If I knew, things would have ended differently."*

*His eyes grow wide, like she has just given him the best news of his life. Her eyes match his, but carry with them a look of confusion, amazement.*

*"You broke my heart," he reveals.*

*The moment the words leave his mouth a chill runs down her body. A rush of emotion, unsure what to make of this.*

*"Is there anything I can do to fix it, to get you back?" he questions.*

*Lily just stands there staring at him, not knowing what to say, not even knowing if she has words for this moment.*

*"I'm sorry, I had no idea. I thought you hated me. I don't even understand what is going on, are you being serious right now," she almost begs.*

*He just nods and touches her neck softly.*

*"I wanted you," she admits.*

*"What about now?"*

*"Yes, now too."*

That whole time, all those feelings, all those urges, those desires, everything, he wanted it too. He wanted me too. This guy, totally out of my league, he wanted me and I didn't understand it. I forgot about Amy, who loved him, the girl who was getting his attention, the girl he had wanted to be with, before me. But she was his second choice, and I was there now, and he wanted me. It was so stupid, both of us so blind, so disconnected. And that was it. It changed everything. The moment I admitted I felt the same way, I wanted that too, that opened the door, to a dream world. Wanted to stay in it forever. It terrified me, and I was ok with that.

It was a bizarre twist, some act of god. Exactly what I needed to get over, what I kept thinking I should have been over at this point. The obsessive compulsive, anxiety, confusion, disorganized, voices, whispers, nonsense. Everything just piling up on top of me. I was struggling to breathe and all I had back home was this ridiculous on again off again, stupid, complicated mess. I wanted more than that. And for a moment, this was good, it was so good. But it's all so fleeting, these emotions, and these decisions. One moment the world felt perfect and still, then my insides would spin, fast paced working, planning, destroying. I came undone. It unraveled so quickly. And before I knew it, it was gone. But I'm getting ahead of myself here.

The first few days, living with this discovery, were perfect. Taylor and I clung to each other. I learned about the man he was, his fears, his dreams. I listened, I took it all in, I was infatuated with the idea of him, of us. He told me why he moved to South Carolina from Chicago, the demons he was trying to outrun. The fresh start he needed. He needed to get back on his feet. He needed to get clean, and he did, and he was. He was building his life back, getting ready to move back to Chicago to go to film school. We talked about Chicago, my birthplace. Me going back, going to school there, how in a year

I would be out there, and he would be there, and the possibilities. It sounded perfect, and I was terrified. It all happened so fast, the plans, the decisions, the honesty. He told me he had been waiting so long for me, how stupid he felt, how excited he was when he heard I was coming back, how he put his life on hold, put everything on hold, just in case. He wanted to give it another chance, one more shot, he wanted to know if his love, his lust, whatever it was, if it was unrequited. The funny thing was I had thought about him from time to time after I got back home. It seemed stupid because I thought he was uninterested, and we lived so far apart, and I was too screwed up for that. But here we were, close to a year later, and everything was different. Everything had changed so much, I barely recognized it anymore. I was so damaged at this point, bruised, worn down, and dejected. Whatever piece of me was left, whatever sanity I still clung to, had been so battered and bruised. I put myself thru misery, waiting for someone, someone who kept me at a slight distance, who had the ability to control my mind, my thoughts, and my actions. He could do that, because I gave him the power. It was killing me, I was already half dead before Nathan, and he was destroying me. Ruining me for love. I felt worthless, I was nothing.

Then somehow, on this trip, in this place away from him, away from the problems, away from myself , I found a tiny piece of perfection. I held so tight to it, I didn't want to lose it. For a moment I felt beautiful, I felt special, I felt like I deserved love. It was so twisted, but I thought, maybe, just maybe I was allowed to have happiness for once. We were inseparable for the first part of the week. Learning about each other, infatuated, in awe. But mid week the girls and I had plans. Plans he didn't like, he was against it, and I was torn. He had a past, made a lot of mistakes, and didn't want to go back there. But me, I had so much to learn, so much I thought I had to live. So much I was fighting. Because despite the joy of finding him, of knowing him, it didn't change the demons haunting me from the inside. And those, I still needed to numb those.

That night we did some powerful drugs. The kind that transcend you to another place, make you see the world differently. It was just the girls, Maya, Amy and me. We had it planned before I even arrived. A world they all wanted to bring me into. It was an every now and then, it would be their second time to do it, and they wanted me to join them, they wanted me to feel that with them. I was so torn, so conflicted. Finally something was working out, something felt so right, and I was compromising it. Taylor begged me not to go through with it, to spend the evening with him, or just to stay with them and not participate. He wanted me to be clean, to stay away from the hard stuff. He didn't want me to go through what he went through, the darkness. But it was already so dark, I was so empty inside, and I told him I had to. That I wanted to. That I would be careful, that I would call him, that I cared for him, but I needed to do this. I remember him being so upset with me, so hurt, and I let him be, because I couldn't change it. We didn't talk the entire day, which felt like a lifetime after spending the past three days with him. I was hung up on it for a while, over analyzing it, guilty, thoughts racing, but I let it go, I had to. For the day, I needed to disappear.

That night in the midst of everything, I wrote him a long letter. Pouring my heart out to him. My fears, my hang-ups. I didn't know how to let someone in, I wanted to let him in so bad, I needed to, I had to, but I was terrified. I was overwhelmed by the idea of being loved, of loving, of wanting something, and being able to have it. It was a beautiful concept but I didn't make sense to me. I forgot about the times when things were reciprocated. All I could remember was the rejection. The scars. My heart, in pieces. I was so afraid to be vulnerable. I didn't even know how. That part was always hard, always so complicated. And the one time, the one time I finally let myself go, let myself get hurt, it ate away at me. It was a mess, a disaster, I hated it, but I was addicted to it. Addicted to the pain, the misery. Why did I let myself get to this point. No energy to get back. The voices growing louder, everything just getting louder. So I confessed to him, to this guy that opened his heart up to me, and begged me to come in. I wanted to jump, wanted to fall. And for a moment I believed I could. But I was paralyzed.

The next day, the day after, I waited for Taylor, waited to hear from him. So afraid he wouldn't want anything to do with me anymore. It wasn't until later that evening I saw him again. It was awkward, uncomfortable. It was with a big group of people at a restaurant. Almost impossible to talk, to work through this. I was leaving the next morning, our time, so limited. I pulled him aside, had to talk to him, needed to be near him.

> *A hot summer day, Lily and Taylor sitting clumsily beside each other on a curb in the parking lot. The warmth of the day heating her bare shoulders and warming the cold within her.*
>
> *"What's wrong," he questions as he slides his arm around her waist, pulling her closer.*
>
> *She tugs away slightly, her body tense, her stomach in knots.*
>
> *"Are you mad? I'm sorry for being stupid, for last night. Can you forgive me?"*
>
> *His face ignites in a smile, shaking his head in disbelief. He touches a hand to her face, moving a hair from her lips.*
>
> *"I could never be mad at you."*
>
> *"I was afraid everything changed, I messed everything up."*
>
> *"No," he shook his head.*
>
> *He moves closer and pulls her in to him, kissing her forehead gently.*

*"I just couldn't be there, I just couldn't think about you doing that. You are perfect. My perfect girl, I just don't want you to go through what I went through."*

*She shakes her head, not understanding the words coming out of his mouth, not grasping what he is seeing in her. Doubt slipping into her mind.*

*"I wrote you this last night," she says as she hands him the letter. He looks down at it, and hands it back to her, "Read it to me."*

*Lily hesitates for a moment before opening the letter. He wraps his arms firmly around her as she pours out her soul to him.*

Something changed in me, so suddenly, the glimmer of hope, the flash of happiness, of chance, of excitement. It vanished. I could feel it leaving, I wanted to grab it back, tug at it, pull it. And it was gone, and the depression set in. I felt myself trying to scream, I wanted to pull my insides out through my stomach. I wanted to rip myself wide open. I wanted to bang my head on the asphalt and roll around until it released me, the monster gripped me, suffocated me, I couldn't breathe. Everything was black, cluttered and loud. I felt his touch on my skin, but it felt so far away. I tried to reach for it and I couldn't. I sunk deep, deep down. And I was gone.

I finally remembered him saying, *a penny for your thoughts.* I vaguely remember looking over at him, shaking my head, unable, or afraid to speak. I knew once I opened my mouth I would be pushing him away. "No, you can't have happiness, you can't have this." The monster screamed inside me. I wanted to cry, but there were no tears. There was numb, there was hate, there was frustration, but there were no tears. He pulled me into him, and this tiny flutter in the pit of my stomach tried to move, a tiny spark ignited, then nothing, it was gone. I went limp in his arms, and he just held me. I didn't have the words to explain this to him, I wanted this last day. I wanted something good. I wanted him, and now I couldn't have him. Impossible. I tried to fight against it, but I was too weak.

Later, driving back to Maya's house he rode in the car with us, he wanted to spend the last night there, with me. I tried to muster up something inside of me, I must have looked like a zombie. He pulled me close and whispered to me, *please let me into your heart.* He was practically begging me. He needed something good, something real. I could sense the desperation in his voice, he wanted more than anything, for me to let him in, to give him a chance. Everything I said was negative. How it couldn't work, why. I focused on everything that would go wrong. The age difference, the distance, him working through his stuff, me incapable of opening my heart. He reminded me of the positives. Me graduating in a year, him moving back to Chicago, us together. Working through this together. He told me I was the best thing that ever happened to him. He thought he didn't deserve me, didn't deserve something good, someone so good. I didn't understand, in my mind I was far from good, on top of all the things I got into, I was broken, I was a mess. I was not good. But in his world I was fresh, I was a change, I was his reward for changing, for trying, I was his prize, a chance for redemption. I was his hope. I didn't understand that, couldn't comprehend it. I needed time, needed more time there. I needed to get my mind back to where it was before, when I believed in something, for a brief moment, when I believed him. But that was gone and I didn't know how to find it again.

I told him how scared I was. I apologized for shutting down, for breaking down, but I couldn't help it. It felt so impossible to get out of this mood, this depression. We spent the night talking. Sitting under the stars. Me on the hood of a car, and him beside me. He talked, I listened. I processed, I analyzed. I screamed at myself inside, to just let go. To unclench everything, to release. I just wanted this last night to be perfect. But this was as close to perfect as we would get. And I hated myself more by the second.

The next morning he came back over. He wanted to go with us to the airport, he wanted to be with me a little longer. It was good to see him. I was amazed that he came back. Maybe I wasn't as bad as I thought, but for whatever reason he was there, waiting for me. Then it was the airport, then it was me leaving, then it was me not even hugging him goodbye, no kiss, no embrace, nothing. I wanted to look over my shoulder and watch him as I walked away, but my concrete heart wouldn't let me. I hated it, and I hated myself at that moment, and all the hours on the flight. I hated myself for running away. But, he had my number, and I told him to call me before he went back to Chicago. I was going to look at colleges in a month, and he would be back. We talked about meeting up, about seeing each other. It was my second chance, my third chance. I would make it right this time, I had to.

He called one night, a few days before he moved. We talked for a while, about his move, about my trip, about where we would meet, when I would see him. How we could make it work. It all seemed so possible now that I was away from it. I felt ready now, I already had a second chance and I felt like I blew it, but he was still there, still ready, still waiting. And I was ready. I had time to think, time to get out of those moments, and I was ready.

We talked about the plans on the phone that night. I gave him numbers to call me at, I emailed him information. He had everything. And as time got closer, I hadn't heard. He was supposed to call when he got to Chicago, he was supposed to call once he got settled. We had these plans, and I was waiting on him. I called Maya and she was shocked I hadn't heard from him. She said I was all he talked about, that he couldn't get me off his mind. I was all she heard about before he moved. Him seeing me, his dreams, his plans. Everything. She didn't have a number, he was supposed to call them, was supposed to contact them when he got to Chicago, when he got settled. I kept holding out. I kept waiting. So convinced he would call, he would find me. Reach me. What could have changed, I didn't understand. I got worried, anxious, angry, scared. I was there, out in Chicago for a long weekend, and I never heard a word. I came home, broken. I thought I was broken before. I thought I couldn't get much worse. I had fought to rebuild myself, to put the pieces back together so he and I could be something, have something. And nothing, there was nothing. No contact. I was speechless. Shocked. Confused. I was so alone. I was numb. I was empty. Back down again, unable to get back up.

It wasn't until much later I got word from Maya. Someone in the Carolina group had talked to Taylor, finally heard from him. He fell apart, he relapsed. Went straight back to the same old circles, the same group of friends he moved across the country to escape, straight back to cocaine. He screwed up immediately after getting back. He was a mess, he was a disaster. He told them he couldn't call me, that he refused to call me. He was so ashamed with himself. He got back into it bad, and I was so good, I was perfect to him, I was on a pedestal and he didn't want to mess me up. He didn't want to mess up my perfection. I hurt for him, for his mistakes, for using, but I hated him for never telling me. Never contacting me. Never again, I never heard from him ever again. He couldn't live with himself for what he let himself become, and he hated himself for losing me. I just wish he could have told me. Broken. Me, always broken now. Always a mess. Clinging on for dear life. Just let me go, let me die.

## Chapter 33

## *i'm pretty sure it was black.*

I got lost in myself. A this point, I didn't really have the energy to fight it. I remember trying to appear *okay, normal* at home, to avoid any questions. The rest of the time I was a zombie. Going through the motions. My doctor was worried about me, concerned. I didn't want to talk. Didn't have anything to say. It was hopeless. Nothing really mattered at that point. Somehow I managed to stay afloat in my classes. I was in the honors clubs, I was taking challenging classes, and somehow I got by. I excelled, succeeded. I didn't know how because all of that was a blur. I had gone up and down so many times, and now I was stuck here. Down.

I had been on an anti-depressant for a while, but it wasn't working. My doctor switched me to something else, some other little pill that did nothing, then she discussed having me get a second opinion. She wanted to make sure she wasn't missing anything. She was pretty sure it was more that just major depression. There was something else in there. Something that would explain the whispers, the impulses. She thought schizo-affective, or bipolar. She wanted more input, needed someone to double check me. Look me over. Figure me out. We read the descriptions together, broke things down. Everything was adding up, all the signs pointing to an explanation. It made me sick. After all this time. All these meetings. All this life I spent in pain, lost, confused, alone, and miserable. We were coming to something, we were finding the answers. It took so long to get there, so long for her to see, to understand, because most of our meetings consisted of me not saying a word. From time to time I would describe something, try to explain something, but I'd get frustrated and I'd give up. She wanted me to set up an appointment with her office mentor. She wanted to move forward. She gave me her medical book to take home, to study, to read, to contemplate. I was so numb leaving her office. The terms, the words, the diagnosis spinning through my head. And I knew right away. The flash covering over me, it was so clear. My mind went back, flashed back to all the times, the moments, these things, and everything was adding up. It was like a death sentence. This cloud hanging over my head.

I drove to the only place I could think of. I went to that apartment. Nathan's apartment, the stupid boy, the place that haunted my dreams. It had been a while. I had moved on with my life. I had been broken again. But I had to go there, I couldn't breathe, couldn't think straight. He was home, he welcomed me in. My mascara, black beneath my eyes. He was what I needed him to be at that moment. Concerned, focused, in tune. I told him about my doctor, about my session. The words, the things she threw out, the things she wanted me to digest. Him, a bipolar mess, chaotic, miserable. And I was terrified. I knew I was screwed up, I knew I had this monster inside of me, I knew I had these things I couldn't explain, couldn't find the words for, these urges, desires, need to run, confusion, cloudiness. These whispers, were they voices, was I hearing these things, something pushing inside of me. I already knew these things, already knew something was wrong, but giving it a possible name, a possible explanation. My life ended at that moment. I felt myself floating overhead. I didn't know why I was so scared. What I thought she would say. Part of me hoped it was all in my head, it was nothing, and it was some relationship sickness. But things were falling into place. Things were fitting, were making sense in the context of the disorder, the disease. Later in my doctor's big medical book, I read the descriptions and I knew right away, which one was me. Maybe not, maybe she was wrong. Maybe it was wrong.

I cried with Nathan for a while. Curled myself in a ball on his floor and he stroked my hair. He told me it would be ok. That they could test me, they could figure things out, not to worry, not to over think it. There were the thoughts of a pill everyday, a pill forever. Yes, this was my death sentence. As miserable as I already was, somehow a name changed everything. I was scared of my own shadow.

I left after a while. I felt nothing for him. I was already broken, and I felt nothing. But I needed to tell him, needed to confide in him. Because he, of all people, he would understand. He did what I needed. He comforted me. We didn't talk about us, we said nothing. I didn't bring it up because it was the furthest thing from my mind, I was through, and I was done. I had moved on. I was broken. I was nothing.

I stayed in the zombie state for a long while. I spent my time scribbling my thoughts, my fairytales, and my chaos into notebooks. Piling it all up, one day I could reference it, one day, I could remember those moments. Leaving some legacy for after I was gone. I felt like I was on the last leg. I thought if I didn't wake up, if I never woke up, I would be released. I went back to my doctor at some point and she made it official. She named me, she branded me. A bipolar mess, manic depressive chaos. A big X covering over me. She wanted to find medications, she wanted to get me set-up, wanted to help, wanted to walk me though it, get me through this. I was numb. And I never went back again. I ran out of the anti-depressant which was okay, because I shouldn't have been taking it alone anyway. It should have been mixed. It should have been balanced out. The impulsions, the on's and off's. The I need's. The obsessions. All there, all present, intensified, increased. She could help fix it, balance me. But I walked away. She handed me a death sentence and she offered me options, and I just walked away. I didn't need it, I would be fine. She was wrong. Everything would be fine. I racked my brain, trying to figure out how to get to the naive place, the place where none of this was real, where I could still push it all away inside. Fight it, fight the creature inside of me. I had some strength left. And I pushed it down. I would get to it later. I didn't have time now. I had to finish. Had to graduate, had to get out of this hell. If I just moved on, if I just got away, it would all change. It was locational, it was fleeting, I told myself it was so, and so it was true.

I wanted to get out. I wanted to fly. Tear up some stretch of road and disappear. I thought if I could just get away. If I could just get out of here things would change. Everything would be different. And I had built this up in my mind so much, it was over taking me. These ideas, this vision, this dream of getting away. And it was all I could imagine. Dreaming. Plotting. There was a place away from here. Away from myself. If I could just get there. If I could only get away, out of myself. Out of my mind. Then this mess I was living in. This disaster. This misery that rocked me out of my sleep, kept me up at night. All those things, they became my constant thoughts. I envisioned where I would go, where this world would take me and occasionally I felt some peace. I felt a quiet. And then a whisper would come and knock me out of myself. It would creep up inside of me, and leave me speechless. I had to get out. I wanted to go. Wanted to run. I hated the waiting. I hated this.

## Chapter 34

# the last leg.

It was senior year. I was a basket case. I was disconnected, focusing all my attention on finishing. My group of friends. We were inseparable. We had worked so hard to get to this point, and most of us had a light load of classes, for all the sweat we poured into the past three years. More free time. More freedom. I was stoned every day. Sometimes a few times a day. I was leaving school, coming back. I was trusted. I was a good girl. I was a fraud. I played it safe for so long, and even though a part of me still cared, I had the freedom to let myself go a little. And so I did. I was silently battling the diagnosis. I was self-medicating since I walked away from treatment. I was all over the place. When I was down, I was a mess. I was unable to function. I called it forced functioning. You did what you had to do because you had to do it, but you had no recollection of it. It was a catastrophe. When I was up, I was all over the map. I was fighting the impulses. I was back seat make-outs, I was spending every dime I had. Part time job, *broke*. I wanted to care but I didn't. It felt normal. There was nothing wrong with me, I was just like everyone else. The irony was I had spent so much time, just wanting everyone to see I was broken, hurting, in pain, and now it was everything I could do to play the normal card. I didn't want this.

I think I had a crush on every guy that year. I knew it didn't matter, couldn't do the relationship thing. I was out of there so fast and I didn't want anything to hold me down. So I freed myself. I released myself. I fell in lust with everyone that crossed my path. One week I was head over heels for one guy, and it changed so quickly. I couldn't keep up with myself. I didn't even care. I just wanted to smoke. I wanted to drive around and listen to music with my friends. I wanted to live my life, I wanted these memories. We did it all, all the things we had talked about, wanted to do, all the moments. We had those. But it wasn't enough. I was a mess, but I played it off. I needed more, but I inched my way through it.

Then one day they broke up. Nathan and Melissa. They finally ended it and we were all overjoyed. It was a miracle. We had her back, and we didn't have to hear the complaints. For a minute I thought about him, about calling, about getting back in touch. But I pushed the thought out of my head. There was so much going on, so many things I had to do, had to finish, had to experience. I wanted my friends, no relationships, none of that stupid crap that distracts you. I wanted to be free. I wanted anything but a relationship. I was already halfway to Chicago, and I was made of stone. Nothing was getting in.

It was almost over. I felt alive. It was stupid, because it was all medicated, it was all destructive. But it was better than the empty void. But that always came back. I'd come down, and it would all come back. I needed to slow it down, but I was so afraid of feeling anything. I hated myself.

# Chapter 35

## this wasn't the plan.

I met him in one of my classes. Jason. He was a junior, a year younger. He was beautiful. We were complete opposites. He was not the kind of guy I would end up with, he was not the musician, he was not for me. He was the guy the girls drooled over. I wasn't looking, but I was noticing. I was noticing him, and I was, *bad accident can't look away*. I was tongue-tied. It was stupid. I didn't need this right now. I needed to get stoned, and not feel, and dream about getting away. I needed to scream at my parents, I needed to react, I needed to stop internalizing every detail. I needed to explode, but I did not need this.

We started talking in class. And it was weird. Awkward, but in a good way. It was flirtation, it was desire. It was *what the hell am I doing* crazy. It was *no strings attached please*. It was stupid. It was playing with fire. But it was butterflies, and it was emotions, and it was a cure for the numbness, and I swayed myself, I stepped too close, almost fell off the ledge. I teetered over the side, I tiptoed around the edges. My heart skipping a beat. This was different. This was maybe real, but every time the flame rose up, I drenched it, poured water over it. My heart, skipping, turning, spinning, and I pulled out the coils, the gears, and the wheels.

He was gentle, sweet. Innocent. He was funny, sincere. He was stupid beautiful. He was hurt your eyes to look at, in a good way, in a bad way. This was stupid. What an idiot I was. I should have stopped myself. I tried. I fought it. Kicked it down. Rung it out. He kept coming back, kept pursuing. I didn't really believe him, didn't believe it, it seemed so crazy. Unbelievable. Unfathomable.

I felt like I was in fifth grade, the time the boy I thought was cute asked me to be his girlfriend over the phone. I said yes. We rode the same bus and in the morning, I didn't sit by him, he was in ear shot, and my paranoia kicked in.

> *A bright yellow school bus picks up Lily in front of her house and chugs along down the road. She makes her way toward the back of the bus. A sweet boy with soft features and a stunning smile watches her as she walks. Lily puts her head down and takes a seat a few rows ahead of him. A friend leans to the boy and whispers.*
> *"I thought you said she was your girlfriend?"*
> *"Whatever, man, shut up."*
> *Lily sinks in the seat and closes her eyes tightly.*

Him saying something about me being his girlfriend. Me misinterpreting it. I automatically assumed it was negative. Act cool, don't get hurt. So I broke it off the next time I saw him. Told him I didn't want to be his girlfriend. That's how I felt. Now, with Jason, that was the paranoia in me waiting for the other shoe to drop. Me not sure what to say, what to do, what to think. I didn't believe him, how could I.

We started writing letters. It was so innocent. I loved the innocence. I was so destroyed. So tainted. So beaten, batter, bruised. An emotional train wreck. I needed middle school romance, check yes or no. I needed simple. But nothing about this was simple, because the closer we got, the more frequent these notes, these letters got, I kept reminding myself, I was gone, I was leaving and I was already halfway there. I didn't need this. I didn't want this. I couldn't allow myself to get stuck, get trapped, to get involved. I had a bad track record as of late. So used to the girl breaking the hearts. Never too involved, never in too deep. I wanted to be that girl again. But I was scared. I was broken, I was a mess.

I would have these ridiculous conferences with my best friends. Me torn between the possibility of an adventure, and the idea of getting roped in too deep. I wanted no strings attached. I didn't want a relationship. Finally, for the first time in a long time, I just wanted to be alone. I wanted to breathe in what I had left, before I got out of this town, away from all these things. At this point I was completely convinced my life, my emotions, they were all situational. If I was positive, if I didn't let everyone get to me, the pressure to succeed, and the distractions. If I stayed focused, if I kept my cool, rode those out a little more, then I would be home free. I truly believed it, and at the time, I didn't have much reason to think differently. It was sort of like when my mom told me they were just teenage problems, they would pass. Well maybe they were mother problems, father problems, boy problems, sibling problems, middle-child-syndrome. What if that's all it was. It gave me hope, something to set my sights on. The idea of Chicago, my sanctuary. My escape. My freedom. No matter how bad things would get, could get, I had Chicago, and that gave me peace. So I'd sit there with my friends, doing the pros and cons the back and forth. Not really truly knowing what was going on with Jason. I just knew I had these letters, these cute letters. They were smart, funny, and simple. I'd scribble in my notebook, some prose I'd put in a letter for him. And this went on and on, back and forth for a while. Me wondering what we were doing, what was happening. This was so new. It felt like someone was courting me, it was a breath of fresh air. The part of me that kept asking "Why me, what does he see in me?" It started to quiet down. My friends were pushing me to take the chance. *You only live once*, they kept saying, *so what if it hurts to go, so what if it's great, don't think about the months of time ahead, just focus on right now.* I knew they were right, but I was still stuck, stuck in this dizzying back and forth.

I made up my mind one autumn day. I seemed to always make my most important decisions when the leaves were falling. I cringed for a moment remembering my vulnerability with Seth, wishing I could take it back or be back there, I'm not sure which. It was a crucial season. The leaves, the colors, the gentle breeze. It was the best time to plan the course for the rest of your life. I wrote it all down in a letter, a beautiful poem. I wanted to continue this back and forth with Jason, it was a game, and I loved playing it. But I thought it out, I wanted it to be special, I was nervous. I was anxious. I was making a huge decision, and I was shaking when I asked him if we could talk.

*Lily and Jason walk side by side in a school parking lot. The sun is going down, the leaves orange and yellow and red, cover the ground. Lily wraps her arms around her body and the breeze blows through her hair, kissing her skin.*
*"Why don't we sit in my Jeep?" he suggests.*
*He opens the door like a true gentleman and waits for Lily to climb in and get situated before closing it for her. She holds a piece of paper folded in her hands, her eyes dart around nervously absorbing her surroundings. After Jason climbs in, he slides his key in the ignition and a warm burst of air hits their faces. Lily rubs her arm gently, warming her cool skin.*
*"So," he attempts to start a conversation.*
*"Yeah, so, this is your car."*
*"It's a classic, I'm sure you can tell," he says as the heater knob falls off into his hands.*
*"I've always loved the classics," Lily smirks.*

*They sit in silence for a few moments, both processing, making sense of where they are, what they're doing.*

*"So, what are we doing?" Lily questions.*

*"Sitting in my car," Jason forces out, unsure of what she is getting at. Not knowing how to turn it off, get serious.*

*"I just need to know what we are doing here. We write these notes, it feels like we're flirting, like we are getting somewhere. I just, I don't know what's going on, what you are thinking, I just need to know."*

*He's quiet for a few moments, watching her. He smiles, coolly before he opens his mouth to speak.*

*"I like you, I like getting to know you."*

*"Can I read you something?" Lily asks, her voice almost shaking.*

*"I watch you from across the room. All eyes on you. My beating heart, skipping in tune with you. Our eyes almost meet, a steady, building heat, I just want to be in tune with you. Don't want to be away from you." Lily reads the words scribbled on the paper.*

*"Okay, I know it's kinda dumb, I guess I like you too, I want to get to know you. I'm not good at this stuff."*

*Jason reaches his hand over to her, touches her flesh, igniting her.*

*"Let's do it," he urges.*

*"But, I'm moving this summer, I'm graduating. This can't be serious, I can't get attached. You have to promise me you won't fall in love with me, please," she begs.*

*"Sure, whatever you say," Jason laughs, only half listening, mostly just spinning with excitement, a fire burning within him. He has her, she's his. He feels he has waited forever for this moment.*

*"Okay, I should go, it's getting late," she says as she stares out at the now dark sky.*

*Jason walks her to her car. She opens the door to get in, they quickly turn back around, and she is face-to-face with his beauty. The moon and stars shining down on them. Her eyes, her face, her breath so close to him she can feel his heart beat. She stands on her tip-toes and kisses him gently on the lips, a surge of electricity flowing between them.*

So we started something, slowly. It was his way of easing me into this relationship I was not ready for. He promised we could take it slow, no titles, just get to know each other. We made a commitment to getting to know each other. But the thing was, it was more than that. I wanted to call him my boyfriend, I was giddy, and he was so different from what I had been used to. But I wasn't ready to say that and I knew my track record, and I knew I needed to be patient, let it fall into place. No one knew there was something between us, it wasn't that we were hiding it, it was just, that we weren't ready to call it what it was. Our closest friends knew, but it was so early, so innocent. No one would have expected it. Complete opposites. Him – the extrovert, the school spirit kind of guy, the dreamy, daydreaming kind of guy. Me – the sullen, creative, music, didn't care girl. No one would have guessed it, would have paired us. A chance meeting, circumstantial. But apparently there was more, there had always been more. There was a past, there was a crush, a desire. He had seen me, thought of me, and longed for me back in those middle school days. I didn't know him then, but he knew me. How strange, the truths you find out. I was so consumed in my stuff, my fears, and my mind shrinking, breathing and swallowing me whole. And even then he saw me. So later, when he found me, when he had me, when I was his, it was something indescribable for him. An impossible thought. I didn't get it, didn't understand. Didn't want to. That would have taken me admitting more than I wanted to. I fought the feelings, kept him at a distance. He didn't keep his end of the bargain. He fell hard and he fell fast.

When we finally made it official, we were sort of at a standstill. He had girls pursuing him, girls that thought there was more. That's the problem when you have this easy-going personality, everyone falls for you. We couldn't hide it anymore, couldn't go on pretending it was nothing. We called it dating, but it was not dating, it was just us. So it slowly spread, broken hearts, girls hated me. I sort of loved it. Sort of loved being hated. Finally I had the upper hand, it was nice.

This was carefree, it was easy going, and it was light. It was me keeping myself just close enough to feel the tingle, but far enough to stay safe, to keep myself so safe. No broken hearts, not this time. This boy, he would not break my heart. He couldn't, because I would not love him. I was so tired of love. I wanted fun, I wasn't easy, I wanted my space, and I wanted things my way. I was impossible to deal with, I was bossy, I was mean, I was *the don't fall in love with me* girl. I was the *I'll break your heart* girl. I was the *so tired of feeling like crap, I need to feel alive* girl. And he was the, *never dated a smart girl, never knew there was this*, guy. It was an interesting pairing, but it was nice. It was good. I tried to keep it simple, I didn't want complicated.

The free time was me and my friends and the drugs, and the college applications, and the ACT's and the SAT's. It was late nights, long weekends, it was cramming, studying, goofing off. It was picture perfect. A lot of the time. But I was moody, I was irritable, I was angry, I *was one minute okay* girl, the next *screaming at the top of my lungs, losing my mind, crazy* girl. I was inconsistent. One day I felt like I was falling in love, and the next day I was in hell. I was *avoid my boyfriend, flirtatious* girl. I was a spinning top. I was a flip of the coin. So scattered.

Then he blew it, he ruined it. He started telling me he loved me, said he couldn't help it, said he had fallen, so hard. He tried to change the rules, wanted me to love him back. But I told him I couldn't, that I wouldn't. I had dreams, I had plans,

I had it all planned out and he wasn't a part of it. I wasn't *home for summer college* girl, I was *the move across the country never come back* girl. I was the *break your heart and never look back* girl. I begged him not to love me, because I was going to leave, that wasn't going to change. He was insistent, but I didn't bend.

## Chapter 36

## something's gotta give.

Aside from Jason falling in love, things were going relatively well. I was dizzy inside, but when it all felt like too much to bear, I closed my eyes and thought of Chicago, and there was a little bit of peace. The days would build up on top of each other, the moments that were too hard to bear, and at night I would cry myself to sleep. I would sob, silently, the pain, so strong, eating away at me. It was my secret. But most days, I couldn't hide it. The relationship was good, keeping a ten foot pole between us emotionally. His love was comforting, but it wasn't my salvation. The bad days were impossible. The moods. The trying to trust people, being let down. It was so risky, living, feeling, I didn't want to. It was stupid, I know now it was stupid, but I wanted to save myself, and I wanted to save him, because I really cared for him, and I didn't want to hurt him.

It was about a month into us officially being a couple when I ran into Nathan at some show, somewhere. Somehow he heard, found out I had a boyfriend, the first official boyfriend since him. He gave me dagger eyes, his anger boiling over.

*Nathan, the tall, thin, unwashed musician with anger burning inside of him corners Lily outside a crowded club. He looks down on her, his eyes, hurt and confused, but mostly angry. Lily is small, shrinking beneath him. Her dark, sad eyes look up at him, into his.*

*"So, you have a boyfriend," it's not really a question.*

*"Yeah, how are you?" she tries to avoid the topic.*

*Nathan just shakes his head and laughs.*

*"Really, how am I, that's all you can say?"*

*"Nathan, what do you want me to say? You start the conversation off with accusations, we haven't talked in forever."*

*"Yeah, exactly."*

*"What do you mean 'exactly'? You were dating one of my best friends and telling me you wanted me. But you told me nothing could happen, I had to keep my distance, what do you expect?"*

*"You told me you would wait, I told you it would take some time. I told you I needed time to let things end, I told you I loved you, told you I wanted to be with you, I told you to wait for me and you said you would."*

*"I can't even have this conversation with you. Wait? I waited almost a year for you, you showed no sign, I just, I can't do this." Lily storms off.*

*"Whatever," he mumbles under his breath, clearly not seeing anything other than his pain.*

Me moving on. His brain couldn't comprehend the hell I went through. He only saw himself. Only saw his pain. I was so afraid I would become him. It didn't make sense to him. All he could see was me not waiting, me moving on, and he couldn't grasp that. He couldn't make sense of it. But I didn't care anymore. I didn't care because I really had moved on. Finally. And I had broken him. I hurt him back. All the pain he caused me over the years, and I stabbed it, right back into him. It wasn't intentional but that didn't mean it didn't feel good. I finally got to break his heart.

Nothing is ever as easy as it seems. I was still me, I still went out, still went to see music, still hung around the same crowd, which meant I saw Nathan, would see him out, see him places. Talk about cold shoulder, talk about daggers, let's talk about it, let's not talk about it. Let's pretend it's fine, like nothing ever happened, like there was never anything there. He would turn his back to me in a group of people. I was nothing to him. And honestly, I really didn't care. Not then, not yet, I was content, and I was with someone that treated me like I mattered. Even when I felt like I was nothing, which was most of the time, Jason made me feel like a human being. I hadn't felt human in so long, it was strange, I loved it.

Things were getting more and more serious with Jason. He told me he loved me every chance he got, and I would just put my head down. I would grab him and tell him, I couldn't say it back, that I couldn't love him, that I wouldn't let myself. He told me he didn't care, he said he would say it anyway, would say it even if I never said it back. Was he demented? I didn't understand him, didn't get it. I couldn't figure out how he could love me so much, say it all the time, love me without hearing me say it, without having his love received or returned. And he didn't change, his personality, his carefree nature, his playful spirit, his innocence, he didn't grow bitter, didn't stop. It felt impossible. Something had to be wrong with him, to put himself through that, to fall in love with someone who swore she'd never love him back. Either he really didn't care, or he was just waiting, waiting for me to let my guard down, waiting for me to fall in love. He was so confident, so sure of himself, of his feelings. Things were nice when we were together, but I wasn't ready yet, I wasn't ready to feel.

I needed to get rid of the baggage, get rid of the stupid boy, of Nathan, weaving in and out of my life. I was seeing him more, running into him, he was attached, seeing someone, but he was so strange with me. So mad at me, and still sort of waiting for me to change my mind. He wasn't serious, he was biding his time, and he was there. He started calling, starting prying his way into my life. Asking questions, too many questions. Trying to get into my head. And he was getting to me, I hated that he was getting to me. He still had the ability to push my buttons, even though I had no desire to be with him, he could still hurt me. He could still belittle me. I was miserable around him. Every time I'd see him, I hated myself. He called a few times for rides, to hang out, and I did because I wanted to try to be friends. I asked him if we could be friends, if we could get to that. He wasn't sure. He wanted to, he said he did. But this, this didn't feel like a friendship. This felt like bitterness, this felt like misery, and he was bringing me into it. Me, always finding a way to kill something good. Me with this great guy, this sweet guy, this non-musician, non-self-obsessed guy, and I was playing with fire. Letting this idiot get to me. It had to stop. He was hurting me, he was messing with me, guilting me. After all we had, after the promises. He kept going back to that, kept focusing on me, not keeping my word. Screw him.

I knew if Nathan couldn't be my friend, if all he could do was guilt me, accuse me, hate me, if all he could offer was his misery, I couldn't take it anymore. We made plans to meet, I told him we needed to talk, needed to clear some things up. So I went to his apartment, to settle things.

*The dark apartment cast a shadow on the mood. Nathan is lounging on a couch in his bedroom and Lily sits down beside him. Awkward, uneasy, both parties silent.*

*"So, can we be friends?" Lily asks breaking the silence. He doesn't really answer, which should tell her what she needs to hear, but she's hopeful, naïve.*

*"Could you be happy with that, with friendship?" she pushes.*

*"I don't know," he says with more of a shrug than words.*

*"You kept me waiting forever, I waited, I tried, I did, but I couldn't do it anymore."*

*They sit there in silence in the dark room, just a crack of sunlight streaming through the windows. Nathan's mood is sullen, downcast. The couch almost swallowing his body whole as he sinks deeper down into it. Lily stares at him intently, tears streaming slowly down her cheeks.*

*"I wish there was a way to make this work, to be in your life, I really do care about you, I always have. If you can't be my friend, I just can't see you anymore."*

*Nathan's eyes are glassy, which catches her a little off guard in the moment. Their eyes clinging to each other, to this moment, not knowing if they will ever be here again.*

Maybe he was a jerk for what he put me through. I knew I helped do it to myself, I knew I gave him the power, but all I wanted was for him to say he was wrong too. That this place we were now wasn't all my fault. I wanted him to admit that and I wanted to know we could be friends. That he could be okay with me, with my decisions. And he couldn't. It was like a break up. He was depressed, and he wanted me to save him, help him, fix him. He wasn't going to get to me. I was in a good place. Ok, well maybe it wasn't a good place, but I had a sweet boyfriend who loved me, who wanted to make me happy. My mental state was unchanged. Well, maybe worse, maybe more scattered, but it was a whole hell of a lot better than where I was with Nathan. Where I let him bring me. I was afraid to get close to him, afraid he could still get to me. And he could. Not in a me trying to love him way, trying to make him love me, the way it was before. But he was a manipulator, he was a guilt trip, a bastard. He pulled and he pushed and he blamed me, accused me. Even then in that room, as I walked away from him. As I told him he couldn't have me, could never have me, even then he broke my spirit, made me question myself. My relationship, my commitment. Because me, stupid me couldn't even bring myself to love Jason, this great guy who courted me, who stood up for me, who wanted me. I felt incapable of love, it terrified me. I had allowed some vulnerability in the past, and I had to be tough now, had to keep my guard up, couldn't feel, couldn't get hurt. I had no time for it, I had bigger plans. And I was face to face with my future. And I walked away, walked out of that dirty apartment, and I was free. I was free, but I felt terrible. Rotten, dizzy, guilty. Wished I hadn't gone to see him. Didn't want to tell Jason. Didn't want him to question my motives, because even I didn't understand them. I could have just left it alone, but I didn't. I needed closure. And I got it. But at what cost, I wasn't sure.

Chapter 37

the fall.

It was winter. The cold, the dark of the season made everything worse. This was before they really advertised seasonal depression. The lack of sun, cold and dark all of the time, I was unstable. I was weak, I was scribbling my words down. Writing more. Putting to words everything I couldn't say. And every now and then I'd read them aloud at a coffee house open mic. Somehow it was easier to say the words behind a sheet of paper. They sounded beautiful read aloud. Most of the time I didn't realize they came from me. I never really thought about writing, I did it all the time, but, it was so natural, I didn't really realize it was saving me. It was my outlet, my defense mechanism. There was the stuffing. There was the numbness. There was the pushing away, but at least I had my words, at least I had some sort of memory, something to keep track of. Something to make sense of my emotions. My feelings for Jason confused me, fooled me, and sank into me. Everything I couldn't say to him was falling onto the blank sheets of paper. I didn't understand what it was and it scared me. Frightened me.

I was the girl who didn't feel. But really, I was the girl who felt too much. Who had a wild imagination that seeped into me. These powerful thoughts that sat, untouched in my mind. Circling through me, spinning. A hard exterior, but all mush inside. I had to stay strong. I had to hold my ground. Had to hang on to my words, it was all I had left. I was self medicating. I was desperate. I was hiding it. I was doing it alone. I was needing it more. The more I stuffed my feelings the more I needed it, needed the numbness. The blank feeling, the floating. I was growing sick of myself, wanting to pull away from everything, but I was losing a piece of myself to him, and I was too proud to admit it.

I remember it was February. Jason just back from a ski trip, leg in a cast, sort of helpless, but still strong. I watched him intently, amazed by him, noticing him, his battles, his never good enough's, living up to's. I saw him, in a way for the first time. That's when it happened. That's when I fell. My heart stopped and restarted in love. I couldn't believe that I let it get this far. That I let myself get so close. Close but still holding back so much of myself. I would be leaving in six months. It was just enough time to drive myself crazy. To second guess myself. Enough time to run, to get away, to break things off. To end this, and end it fast. I could get over him in a few months, I could bounce back. I could free myself. But this part of me wanted to tell him, wanted to let him know, wanted to respond after he said I love you with something other than silence. I debated. I confessed it to a friend, and once I did, I couldn't stop thinking about it. Obsessing over it, deciding how to act, what to do, to say, if anything. Nothing. I changed my mind, went back and forth, I didn't know how I could look at him, could stare him in the face, knowing. So I did all I knew how to do. I wrote it down, I made it sound magical, beautiful, I confessed it in my prose, and I held onto it, not sure if I should give it to him, show it to him, admit it to him. It shouldn't be this big of a deal, but everything was a big deal. Everything was overly complicated.

It was Valentines Day. We went out for dinner, we kept the conversation light. My heart racing, not knowing what or how, not knowing. This weight covering over me. I stumbled over my words. He questioned me, what was wrong. I seemed distant.  He couldn't be more dead on.  Yes I was distant, yes I was pulling away, scared to admit this.  The words I wrote burning a hole in my pocket.  After dinner I told him I wanted to talk, and his face twisted.  I'm sure it sounded serious, I'm sure it terrified him.   He was ready for me to end things, expecting it.  We pulled off to a spot overlooking the city, and I pulled the folded piece of paper from my pocket.

> *The city is dark beneath the glow of the parking lights.  Jason, ruggedly handsome in the driver's seat stares at Lily, uneasy.  Lily's hands fidget, heat rushing over her as she touches her back pocket where she keeps the letter.*
> *"So what's going on?" Jason wonders.*
> *"I want to read you something," Lily responds without looking up.*
> *Jason grows tense, assuming the worst.  Lily pulls the paper out of her pocket and proceeds to read the confession of her love for him.  She has fallen.  Without stopping to breathe she plows through the prose, when she's finished she closes her eyes and takes in the air around her before turning to look at him.*
> *"Really?" his face erupts in a grin, no use trying to hide it, he just got everything he's ever wanted up to this moment.*
> *Lily reaches her hand over to him and squeezes his arm gently.  She imagines two strong arms wrapping her in, she wants to back peddle the confession but she grows intoxicated just looking at him.  Their bodies both tingling with excitement.*
> *"I love you," he says kissing her forehead, further igniting the mood in the car.*
> *"I love you too," Lily says in almost a whisper and for a moment they had achieved perfection.*

Our lives changed, me admitting love out loud for the first time.  Everything, out in the open.  We spent the next few months in bliss. When we were together, it was good, it was really good. But inside I was breaking down, holding the pieces together.

*Chapter 38*

*the guilt.*

As things progressed in my relationship, things at home were falling apart even more. I was uncomfortable. I was distant. I was hiding. Barely around. Just enough to keep the questions away, but not enough. I wondered if Zoe was okay, if she was empty inside like me. If I was alone. If everyone else in the family was alright, what about Sam? Was it just me, the insane one, alone. Afraid to blow my cover, I just stayed away. Stayed away because it hurt to look at them. I wondered if Zoe would be screwed up. If she already was. She seemed okay, but I still felt guilty. The problem was, nothing changed. I was out of it, I was too busy dealing with myself, and I didn't have the time to take on more. I noticed my little sister's anger. So young, yet so angry. It frightened me, but I mainly ignored it. Mainly set it aside, and got lost in myself.

Everyone played okay on the outside, but I wasn't sure if that was true. Wasn't sure if we were functioning. Dysfunctional. But I figured most families were dysfunctional in their own ways. And I was a masochist. And it all just ate me away inside. Chicago I thought. My sanctuary. I wanted to be good enough, but it was impossible. I was supposed to be perfect, and I didn't know what that meant. I was trying to find some happy medium. Happy, impossible.

# Chapter 39

## the downfall.

The school year was coming to a close, a few months away, I was close to freedom. So close I could taste it. My mouth, salivating, my lips tasted sweet. And it sunk in. It sunk in that I was leaving and I pulled away, slowly I pulled away. Tried not to let anyone notice. The more time I spent with Jason, the more I resented him. I loved him, and I needed to stop. I needed to pull away. I started noticing guys again. My eyes were wandering, my thoughts, leaving him. So distracted. Flirting. Forgetting what I had, how good it was. Hating it. Hating that I loved him. It was ruining things. What was supposed to be light, what started as something simple, it was clouding my thoughts. I slowly inched away from him. He wanted more of me, more time, more focus. He wanted to make the most of the short time we had. He wanted to stay with me, he wanted to try it, wanted to keep me. Wanted me to be his. I refused. I told him we had a deal from the beginning. He told me he never agreed, never held back. Always wanted more, hoped I'd change my mind. No, I couldn't. Pretty soon I would be gone, I needed to be gone.

I did the "high fidelity mix cd's", flirting. I did the playful, I did the crossing the line. Playing with fire. I hated myself for it, but it didn't make me stop. If I could push away, rip myself away. Pull my heart out. If I could think clearly, if I could just

173

get away from him. It was clouding my judgment. I was losing him. And I could feel him, oblivious. Me trying to be sly, me trying. I wanted him to hate me. I wanted him to take back his love, give up on me, and let me go. He didn't fall for the bait. He ignored my bad behavior. Tolerated it. Dealt with it. I didn't want to hurt him, didn't want things to end this way, but it would be easier. I needed solace. I had to think, had to get away.

# Chapter 40

## destined for failure.

It was graduation. It was summer. It was me still with Jason, wanting to make it work. A change of heart. I was still going to walk away when summer ended, but I was ready to hold on until then. I was using him, trying to keep my sanity. Friends moving away, everything changing. And him, consistent. Always there, always loving me. I was stupid, I was hurtful, I was screwing it all up, and he just kept loving me. I was wondering when it would change, when he would start hating me. When this intensity would turn against me. I hoped I was gone by then, I hoped I never had to see it. Never had to face it. I could feel this clash of emotions, but I wasn't ready to lose him.

The change in me, it happened over night. The me convincing myself to hold on, it slipped out of me. I was out with one of my best friends Courtney one day. And I ran into this guy Matt, I had met once or twice before. It was different. It was, new, fresh. It was an out. I started seeing him around more, running into him at shows, at restaurants. I was slipping away. Pulling away from Jason. Infatuation. I wanted this. This new thing. This new guy. My insides were twisting in knots. I had been fighting against them for the past few months, it was harder than normal, and I needed to feed the monster. I needed to run.

Me emotionally attaching to someone else. Matt was older, confident, creative, funny, outgoing, he wasn't drop dead gorgeous like Jason, he was just a guy with a great personality. I kept thinking of all the negatives with Jason, all the things I hated. All of his not good enough's. It was horrible. It was me at my lowest. At my meanest. At my most cruel. I hated his hobbies. His taste in music. His inability to be serious. Always making light of things, of moments. I hated his goofy voice. The way he dressed. His rough hands. His awkwardness. Immaturity. Insecurities. I was dissecting him. Picking him apart until he was nothing in my mind. He didn't deserve this. He deserved a real goodbye. He was beautiful. Smart. Funny. Creative. Loving. Gentle. Amazing. I was dating a saint and all I could see was his faults. He deserved two more months, I should have given him that, but I didn't. It was the monster creeping into my flesh, oozing out of my pores. I could feel it destroying me. Any goodness I may have had, it was being sucked out of me. I backed out. I told him it was better. I told him if we ended it now, it would be easier. I know he didn't agree. I don't know what he thought. What he was thinking. What was going through his head. I should have given him a goodbye. But me, so afraid to love, so afraid to feel, so afraid that staying with him would ruin my plans. So I broke free. Devoid of feeling. I was waiting for him to hate me. He was waiting for me to change my mind, but I moved on so fast. This secret inside of me, this newness, this distraction. So I moved on to Matt. This not even remotely close to my normal guy thing. It consumed me. The stupid obsessions coming back. Pouring myself into this. It felt like so much more then, but it was a lie. Me again, the fraud. But I was getting used to that. I didn't hate myself yet. I was too busy filling myself with some twisted idea of happiness. It was complicated. It was intense. I was insane. Completely insane. And I was running out of time. I thought I was bad before, but it was all just getting worse.

# Chapter 41

## goodbyes.

I was holding on to this Matt thing for dear life. Not really knowing what it was, but letting it distract me. Distract me from leaving. Distract me from the evil thing inside of me. The disease rotting me from inside. I was counting down the days for my departure. My should be boyfriend, Jason, the good guy. He came over to say his goodbyes. A moment in time I wish I could get back. Wish I could do over again.

*Jason, tall and strong leans against the doorway of Lily's bedroom. Cardboard boxes filled the space where there used to be a floor. Lily, apprehensive, keeps a safe distance from Jason. She tries to busy herself with taping boxes as he slowly moves deeper into the small room.*

*"I can't believe you're really gonna be gone," Jason whispers.*

*Lily watches him, trying to be so strong. Not wanting this moment to get to her. She's stronger than this, she can handle this. She's leaving and he means nothing. But deep down she knows he meant everything, he was everything. Her mind keeps reeling back to Matt.*

*"I'm gonna miss you," Jason adds.*

*"I'll miss you too," she says because she thinks she should, but she means it.*

*Jason walks to her and takes the packing tape from her hands. He places it on the bed and holds her for a moment in his arms. Both of their hearts racing violently in the moment. He leans down and kisses her lips gently and holds them there until she pulls away.*

*She tries to fight the tears, but it's no use. Lily hugs him gently.*

*"Bye," Jason whispers in his perfect voice.*

*Lily gives him a subtle nod and watches him walk out of the room.*

He was beautiful as we said our goodbyes, and I hated him for it. And I wanted to hate myself for what I had done to him. For the secrets I kept from him, but I wasn't there yet. I wanted to wrap my arms around him and take it all back, hold on to him just a little longer. But I was so numb, crazier by the minute. My mind spinning.

And there was the guy, Matt. The new guy, the reason I threw so much away. I let him occupy my time, my thoughts. Drove me crazy. He was torn. Wanted me, but he had his own demons, so he couldn't really be with me, it was painful, it was stupid, but it hurt me, and I needed that. That's how I had to break free. That is what I needed to leave. And before I knew it, I was gone. I was out of there. I was full blown running. I was escaping. I was anxious, excited, I was believing everything would be better. A million times better. My new Chapter, my new journey. And I was ready for it.

There are these things you hold onto, they become who you are. They become your story. They are first kisses. First loves. They are the good mixed with the bad, all of these things create you, form you into the person you are, who you will become. But the inability to see clearly, it consumes you. It transforms all of those moments and magnifies them. It intensifies, escalates. Before we realize it, we are gone. And I was gone. I was looking for more than I had. Needing more than I should have, all these lives I met along the way, all the roads I crossed. And in the midst of it all, I closed my eyes, fell backward, and allowed myself to fall. It wasn't perfect, but it was. And it wasn't a write home about it fairytale, but it was a small miracle. Me with my eyes closed. Me in some way letting go. This was a never before, and at the rate I was going it was likely to be a never again. I wasn't really sure what I was after but I was searching. I was bent over backwards looking for something to clear my head. I wasn't used to putting my racing thoughts aside.

But I had a moment of spontaneity. Even with all of my impulses. My behaviors, I still thought, analyzed, and planned these moments. This quiet insanity, this compulsion. Calculating the degree of risk. Assessing the damage. I set my inhibitions free and allowed myself to be released for a moment, in the quiet thoughts it was all so clear. A rush, a gentle breeze, and in a moment it was gone. Vanished. Disappeared. And before I knew it the sounds were back again. And the silence, the peace, it was all gone. I dreamt of having it back again, and then I laughed at the impossibility.

*Part III*

*Chapter 42*

*false starts.*

I was alone. On my own. A new city, a new place. And everything was good, everything was easy. Until it wasn't. It snuck up on me. I felt sort of balanced. I felt the way I told myself I would be. I felt calm, and at peace. For about a month, alone, by myself, distanced. Nothing holding me back. A fresh start. But it wasn't long before the sinking started. I was used to a rush, I was used to it pounding into me, wasn't used to it creeping. It was sneaky, always sneaky, but never like this. Never this slow molasses, this unsure, this unsteady. So slow I barely noticed it. Didn't see it coming until it was too late. I was losing track of time. I was curled in a ball on my tiny living room floor. I was climbing in the shower. No water, in a ball on the shower floor. I was fully clothed, water pouring all over me. I was digging my fingers into my flesh. I was *slow, calculated cuts.* I was *loud whispers.* I was *can't sleep at night.* I was *a flood of emotions.* I was *unable to cry,* I was *lost in the tears.* I was *never leave the house.* I was *afraid to go outside.* I was all of these things. Everything I could never be. Everything I had pushed down, ignored. Unable to crack, unable to let go. I was *a month before college started, figuring out how to pull the pieces together, searching my brain.* Finding nothing. I was *paralyzed.* I was *not eating,* I was *unable to stop.* I was *scared of my own shadow* tired. I was *stay in bed.* I was *a mess.* This didn't make sense to me. I thought I bought into the change of scenery, change of heart, change of mind.

The month dragged on. I rarely left my apartment. I thought I should be making friends, should be looking for a job. Should be getting adjusted to being on my own. Preparing for school. Should be a lot of things. But wasn't. I thought it would get better once classes started. It was just my brain's shock of not really having anything to do for a month. It was my body reacting, my mental state. So used to achieving, striving, accomplishing. It was this strange in between, and I was ready for it to end.

When classes did finally start, I pulled myself together. Just long enough to get through the days. I poured myself into meeting people, adjusting. Who did I want to be? All these ideas of this girl, ready to do anything, ready for everything. I could be any person I wanted to be. This was my chance to scratch the - keep to myself, introverted, crazy, and mean, this was my chance to be carefree, fun, light. The weight dragging me down. I dreamt about the person I could be, become, the transformation. It was perfect, but I couldn't shake off the monster. Couldn't get it to just back off, back down.

I kept to myself mostly. Walked about the campus, soaking in the sunlight. I was free, but I wasn't really free. I had locked myself up, and thrown away the key. Always doomed. One day, walking across the grass commons on the way to a class this guy walked up beside me.

*"You really shouldn't walk on the grass," he criticizes. Lily isn't really in the mood to talk to anyone, and especially isn't in the mood for someone to tell her what she should or shouldn't do.*
*She sort of rolls her eyes at him, hoping he gets the point. He keeps walking beside her, him on the sidewalk, her on the grass.*
*"Were you just sitting by the tree?" he asks.*

*Lily sort of shrugs.*

*"I was over there," he points behind them. Lily doesn't even turn to look.*

*"I was with some friends there, and I saw you sitting alone."*

I remember feeling the stare of someone's eyes on me that afternoon. I always seemed in tune with my surroundings, normally I would have looked, would have checked to see, but I was exhausted. I was distracted. We split in opposite directions. He had a goofy grin on his face when he walked backward in the opposite direction. Telling me how nice it was to meet me, reminding me to use the sidewalk. He sort of annoyed me. All of his questions, I didn't know what he wanted from me. But as I watched him walk away, the butterflies stirred in the pit of my stomach.

As I sat in my last class of the day, we were watching presentations. I was in a daze, seeing his eyes. His dark eyes, they were bright. They were happy. I had never seen eyes like those before. I couldn't stop thinking about him. His eyes, his laugh. I hoped I'd never see him again. All that happiness, I didn't want to mess with that.

## Chapter 43

## *you changed the game.*

Months passed in the blink of an eye. It was almost time to go back home to see my family for the holidays. It seemed like an eternity since I'd seen them last. It was good to have space, distance. I never thought I'd miss my younger sister so much. Still worried for her, about her. Worried about myself. I fought not to think about it, I just wanted to go, put in my time and come back. I didn't even feel like seeing my friends, didn't want to be found out, analyzed, questioned. I had called Jason a few times since I moved. That's when the guilt started to set in. That's when I wished I had done it differently. That's when it really hit me. When we talked, it was always awkward, and it was always him, finally hating me. Me, hating myself. So afraid all the time. Trapped, locked in a cage, begging to be let out, but it was my key, it was me, and it was always me. I thought about seeing him when I went back, thought about telling him I was sorry, thought about doing a lot of things. But I didn't want to go, didn't want to face the past.

I was sitting under a tree on campus, finishing up some reading for a class. I felt eyes on me and turned to see the guy from earlier in the year smiling big at me. My heart skipped, slowly. He walked over and sat down next to me. Introduced himself as Kyle, and I realized I hadn't known his name.

*Kyle with his big goofy grin, heart racing, inability to slow down almost dances in conversation around tired, sluggish Lily.*

*"What's this book?" he asks as he grabs it from her hands.*

*"Women's Health."*

*"Are you majoring in Women's Studies," he almost shouts.*

*Lily shakes her head, not sure what to think or feel in this moment.*

*"Film studies. You?" she finally answers.*

*Kyle plops down beside her.*

*"Wow film, that's so cool, that's what I want to do, but I'm not."*

*Lily just laughs at him, not really knowing what else to do.*

*"So tell me about yourself," he insists.*

*"No, that's ok," she shakes her head.*

*Kyle just smiles at her, bouncing in circles around her.*

*"I have to get to class, nice to see you again Lily," he smiles. His hand brushing gently up against hers as he walks away. Lily's eyes close without thinking, and the weight disappears from her.*

I tingled all over when he walked away. I forgot what that felt like, to have human contact, to be near someone. I hadn't hugged someone in months, I was a hole, an empty tomb, and I was desperate for the interaction. He annoyed me, crowded my space, but he fascinated me. No reservations. Just there. I started looking over my shoulder everywhere I went. Wondering if I'd run into him again, wondering if I'd see him. I wasn't sure why I cared. He wasn't my type. He was whatever. Maybe I didn't have a type. I was clueless.

I didn't see him again before I left town. I half expected I would. It was probably for the better.

## Chapter 44

## *back in it.*

I had four days. Time with family, coordinating with friends. Cramming it all in. All the reservations I had about going home, they vanished. I wanted to do everything, see everyone. I set the plans. I did as much as I possibly could. I soaked up the time with my younger sister. So much I had neglected with her the last four years. I remembered loving her so much before. Then I remember one day, just hating everyone.

I watched Zoe play video games. It was the tiny things. The things I had missed out on before. I wanted some of those things. Zoe, still so young, so innocent.

> *Lily and Zoe walk side by side through a neighborhood. Large grassy yards, families throwing the ball around, dogs roaming. Lily reaches down and takes her hand.*
> *"I just want you to be happy always," tears well up in her eyes.*
> *"I don't want you to ever go through these things I go through," she almost whispers.*
> *Zoe's big eyes stare up at Lily, and she squeezes her hand tight as they continue down the street.*

I wanted that for both of them. Samantha and Zoe. I wanted happiness for them. Even Samantha and I, once so close, our lives growing up together and even her I couldn't be honest with. I wanted for them what I couldn't find on my own. I tried to make up for lost time. I tried to get a piece of my life back. I made the plans, I went against my better nature, and I had coffee with Jason. It was awkward. It was quiet. It was me not knowing what to say, what I shouldn't say. We talked about his last year of high school. My college classes. We talked about the weather, really, we did. The entire time, sitting there with him, all I wanted to do was break down. Apologize. Make up for the crap I put him through at the end, but the thing was, I couldn't. I couldn't go there, couldn't say that, because I was afraid. Afraid he would forgive me, and I would want to have him back, it back. That I would want a second chance. So I swallowed my thoughts, I hugged him tightly goodbye, and left. I should have told him I was sorry, but I wanted to be the monster. I wanted him to hate me.

Leaving was harder than I thought it would be. It should have been easy. It should have been *get me the hell out of here*, but it was quiet. It was nice. I sort of missed them, missed my family, everyone, on their best behavior for the holidays.

## Chapter 45

## *i hated him.*

Back on campus, back in my routine. It was easy to forget what I had left behind at home when I was so busy spinning my wheels. Trying to make the grades, trying to get ahead in my major. Trying to ignore myself. I was functioning, but I was slow moving, I was no energy. I was silence.

I finally ran into Kyle. I guess I had been waiting to see him again, waiting for a conversation. Waiting for an escape from reality. It wasn't what I expected, when I saw him again, when I snuck up on him this time.

> *Kyle is sitting on the steps in front of a large library reading a book. Lily sneaks around the corner and pops out in front of him. "Hey," she almost surprises herself with the excitement.*
> *Kyle doesn't even look up, barely stirs in his spot.*
> *"Hey," he almost mumbles.*
> *"So what are you reading?" Lily inquires.*
> *Kyle looks at the cover of the book in his hands, clearly stating the title, right in front of her. Then his eyes look back at her with an air of annoyance. Apparently that's his answer.*
> *Lily's heart races, her mind stirs.*
> *"Are you okay, you're acting strange."*

*'How would you know, you don't even know me,' Kyle just shrugs at the question.*

*"I'm gonna go to class," Lily says as she leaves in a hurry. She keeps her eyes forward, not looking back over her shoulder to see if he's watching her leave. He is.*

A few weeks later I was in a café on campus studying for an exam. I was nervous, anxious, I was unprepared. I was *why did my damn ipod run out of batteries* distracted. Perfect timing, Kyle sat down across from me.

*Kyle's faced beams into a smile. His eyes bright and clean.*

*"Hey, hope I'm not bothering you," he grins even bigger.*

*Lily's anxiety escalates. Her heart racing and skipping beats all at once.*

*"I'm trying to study," Lily looks back down at her book.*

*"You're cute when you study," he says watching over her.*

*Lily fights the urge to get up and walk away, to scream.*

*"So what are you studying for?"*

*"Exam," she answers without looking up.*

*"Come on, don't you have a minute to spare? I'll get you a coffee," he offers.*

*"No, thanks," she looks up, trying not to get lost in his deep dark stare.*

I wanted to get up, wanted to leave, but I couldn't move. I just sat there. He was mean. I hated him. He fascinated me.

# Chapter 46

## the thing about fire.

As the months went on, I saw Kyle more. Ran into him more. Us, always at odds with each other. Some film debate. Musical tastes. The state of the world. No middle ground. It was annoying, and impossible to avoid. I was sort of hooked, sort of in need of these stupid, pointless moments with him. It didn't make sense. But there wasn't much that did.

School, these moments with Kyle, that was all I really had. The rest of the time it was me, sinking. Me curled in my bed, trying to figure out what to do. Not knowing what to do. One early morning, fog filling the outsides, not enough sleep. I woke up disoriented in the bathtub. Fully clothed, in a ball on the ground. Wet. Cold. Clueless. I didn't remember being there, getting there. I could figure out, couldn't retrace the steps. Something had to change. Something had to shake. It was me, or the monster, it was two to one, it was three strikes and you're out, it was me with the short end of the stick.

On campus that same day, I saw Kyle walking up the steps of the library. I turned in the other direction. Hid behind the building. It didn't make sense. I was avoiding him, I didn't know why, didn't understand. I was a child. I was lost. I felt myself sinking into the side of the building. Slowly sliding down, melting into the concrete. I needed help. I needed something. I didn't know how much longer I could hold on.

I stumbled into the counseling center on campus. Half in an emotionally drunken stupor, half anxious. I had overheard someone talking about free help. Free sounded good. Free sounded like, no strings attached, no parents, no finger pointing. I was *heavy breathing*, I was *racing heart*, I was *someone get me out of my skin*, when I walked into the psychiatrist's office. She was foreign, she was *everything is better with an accent*. I went through my medical history. I described my counseling situations. I talked about the medications I was once on. I talked about not being on them now. I talked about thinking I didn't need them. I told her my symptoms. She was wide-eyed. She was *ready to start a lecture*, mad. And me, I was frozen.

She analyzed it. Told me the antidepressants would never work, that they would have only catapulted me over the edge, increased the mania. Was she agreeing, was she telling me it was true? Was she saying these ups and downs, all the stuff I was running from. These twisted moods. The fiery pit. She was confirming the diagnosis. She was writing the prescription, she was giving me the run down. I was *why is this happening* complicated. She wanted me stabilized. She wanted to see me once a month, she wanted to work on the stuff beneath the surface. She arranged it so I could get free meds and she told me we were going to work on me. I probably should have been relieved. But instead I was, *a pill everyday* crazy. I was *this is the rest of my life* insane.

Me, not ready to deal with the consequences. I had it together. I was perfect on the outside, so far from perfect everywhere else. I projected the I'm ok attitude. I was the, *we don't have to worry about her she'll be fine* child. I was *this is too much pressure* kid. I was the *don't think, just do*. But I was always thinking. Always, nonstop. It was impossible to shut my mind off. At night, when everything was quiet, the calm before the storm. My head spinning. Talking to me, whispering so loud. I would pace around my bedroom at night. I would slam my head into walls. I just wanted to rip it out, rip the monster out. I had the meds. I had the routine. But I was *every other day on top of it.* I was *not ready to take these pills* difficult. I was only hurting myself I thought. No one else had to worry about how I was feeling. It was my decision. Knowing nothing had changed, knowing it was the farthest thing from a phase, but I still stood my ground. I didn't want this to be my forever. I wanted a happily ever after. I wanted a fairy tale story. Instead, it felt like a death sentence.

I went to my doctor, never missed my appointments. We brought things out in the open. She would ask how I was feeling, would ask about the meds. But they weren't working. Even when I got consistent, for a while, I was still everywhere, all over the place. She switched things up and for a month I was shaking, I was twitching. I was uncomfortable. I was crying as I held my body to keep it still. I thought maybe this was my new normal. This wasn't working. I didn't want to take the stupid meds anymore. At all. Nothing was changing, it was only getting worse. It all seemed pointless. I was gaining weight. Stupid pills, stupid weight gain. I was so over it. It wasn't worth it.

## Chapter 47

## game over.

I started seeing Kyle again around campus. I was so beaten down at this point, unsure of what was going on. Doing my classes, and dealing with bad meds, no meds, and more meds. I was alone. Not telling anyone, not sharing this. Keeping this to myself. Kyle stopped me one day on my way to class. He was sweet, asked if we could hang out after class. I agreed to meet him, wasn't really in the mood to be alone.

*Lily walks into the campus coffee shop and scans the room, laptops, and backpacks, books, and folders cover the tables. Kyle is sitting in a corner by himself reading a book. Two paper coffee cups sit on the table. Lily takes a deep breath as she walks to meet him. He looks up from his book as she gets closer, with a grin you would miss if you didn't look hard enough.*

*"I was afraid you wouldn't come," he stands to greet her. Lily just shrugs and takes a seat.*

*"Is this for me?" she asks as she touches the coffee closest to her.*

*He nods and smiles, looking almost pleased with himself.*

*"It's been a while, huh?" he questions.*

*"Well last time I saw you, you were a complete jerk so ya, I guess."*

*"I was?"*

*"It's like you can't make up your mind, one minute you are nice and the next you are a jerk, I don't get it."*

*He turns bright red on the spot, his cheeks warming, his eyes darting back and forth like he's been found out.*

*"Well, I thought if I could get you to hate me, than I could get you to love me."*

*Her heart stirs in her chest.*

*"Kinda stupid I guess," he says with a boyish grin.*

What a twisted thought. This guy was ridiculous, he was weird. He was sort of sweet, sort of beautiful, perfect eyes. I didn't want it, and it worked. His stupid game worked. I did hate him, I hated him so much I wanted to be near him. It was twisted. Unhealthy. Had to change. And he did change. He slowly changed. I could hardly deal with myself and I didn't really know who he was or what he wanted and it all just seemed complicated. I was *the always have a boyfriend, so distracted you don't have to think or feel* girl. And I was *the hurt people, break hearts, not ready to love kind of* girl. I wasn't ready to burn another bridge. I needed some space. Some time to think. But I had a feeling I wasn't going to get that.

We had this standing date. We had these get to know you meetings every Tuesday after my last class. He was already done for the day and he waited around. To talk. To get to know me better. I kept my space. I soaked it all in. I was, *I'm the girl with the problems, I am the girl with the monster inside, and I'm the girl who can't get close, can't love.* He didn't really seem to care. I had to let him know what he was getting into. What this was leading to. He seemed unfazed. Like I was some new adventure, something he could explore. Something he could research, could understand.

He was soft outside, hard beneath the surface. He was his own conundrum. I was into this. I was wanting more. I was over the moon. But it wasn't right. Because I wasn't right. I was skipping my meds. I was, distracted. Thought I was ok, thought I didn't need it. I was *are we really doing this all over again* crazy. I was making poor decisions and I confessed it all to him. It was my saving grace. He was my guardian. He wanted to be with me, wanted to try this, wanted to give it a chance. He was hands on. He was what I needed. What I didn't want. He was good.

I looked forward to our meetings. To these moments we would spend together. Everything around us vanished, us at the corner table, mapping out our dreams with sugar packets. It was sort of beautiful, it was innocence, and it was *hands brushing up against each other, rosy cheeks*. It was *a scribble our names in a notebook* sort of crush, and it was escalating. I was torn. Half of me, not ready, wanting it to stay exactly as it was. But the rest of me wanted to dive in, no reservations. Blindfolded. The only problem was, I didn't think I would float. All the weight inside of me, so heavy, holding me down. I knew I'd crash, I'd land face first.

I started over analyzing everything. Every word from his mouth. Searching for a reason, an excuse to back off, to get the hell out of this. I would pick apart his sentences. I would notice the way he looked at, talked to other people. I would fact check his stories, see if I caught him off guard. Bad short-term memory. When he misplaced things I searched for names, a girl, something. He was clean. But I was paranoid. Obsessive. I wanted to be brave enough to walk away, to tell him it just couldn't work, that we had to stop, couldn't be friends, and couldn't do this. I didn't deserve something good. I tested it, pushed it, wanted him to hate me. Wanted him to leave. If he left, if he walked away, the satisfaction in knowing I was right, I needed that. It was sickening. So ready to destroy everything I came in contact with. I was trying to work through these things, but I was unstable. I was half way there, I was walking backwards. He was getting to me. Had gotten to me. I needed out. I let my crazy shine through, I hardly thought about what I was doing. How I was acting. I didn't stop myself when I thought I was taking it too far. I just let myself go, as much as I was able to. But at the end of the day, after our mini dates in the cafe, he would tell me he'd see me tomorrow, and he was there, every time.

## Chapter 48

## a shot in the dark.

Spring seemed like as good a time as any. To take our relationship out into the real world. I was feeling comfortable in my new life, new place, new school, and new freedoms. I was even enjoying the idea of having someone, being with someone again. So when Kyle asked me out to dinner one evening after coffee, I accepted. And he took me, right on the spot. He told me he didn't want me to back out, to change my mind. Told me he assumed I was prone to running when things got serious. I wanted to wrap my arms around him. I rolled my eyes, sort of laughed. But inside I knew he was right. And I wanted to run so badly. The more I knew him, the more time we were together, everything just got more complicated. I was doing great in my classes, I was making good friends, and I was doing all the things my doctor wanted me to do. But inside, deep in the pit of my stomach, nothing was changing. I didn't understand. All these things I was doing, me trying to be sane, me trying to do normal, and inside, I was a mess. I was a piece of work. He was an angel and I was scum. I was lost. I was so alone. A million people around you alone. He was right there, and I was gone.

He noticed the changes. He thought it was because he moved too fast, took me out too soon. Maybe dinner was a mistake. I didn't really care anymore. The semester's end was fast approaching and he was over analyzing our first real date. The thing was we had already had several more since that first one. But that was the one, that was the one that ruined me. If I could have found the words then to tell him, it wouldn't have been about a night, a date, a moment, it would have been about me falling. No safety gear. No net. There wasn't much he could do about it at that point, even if he walked away, I would have already loved him. But it was too soon to admit that.

Funny that it was *love at first sight*. Funny that he didn't have the *don't talk to me I never want to be in love again* moment. He had the big, bang, I never knew I'd find you here moment. And later he told me, he knew from that first moment. When he saw me lying under the tree reading a book. He knew then, that he loved me. It didn't make sense to me, he was ridiculous. I was looking for an ulterior motive. I was questioning everything. I didn't understand what it was like to just jump in, to be so free. He was way ahead of me. We needed more. Needed to move forward. Push it to serious. But I was impossible. Those times, him so sweet, so beautiful, and I would sabotage it. I found peace in my misery. Some twisted peace. The kind that doesn't really exist.

# Chapter 49

## darkness.

I had laid all my cards out on the table. I gave Kyle the opportunity to walk away, and he stayed. He stayed, and I thought it would just make everything better. Him there, a constant. A shoulder. But I was fighting myself more, and he was holding me tighter. Things would be okay for a little while, but then they would just fall back down. And for a while, it all seemed like it was going to work out. I was actually taking my meds. Well, more than I had been before, but I was so numb inside. Then before I realized it was happening. It slowly collapsed. The bottom fell out from under me.

I was missing classes. Oversleeping. Barely moving, barely functioning. At work, I was a zombie, doing enough to get by. I was sabotaging my friendships. I was pushing everyone away. I was *locked in my room, cut myself to take away the pain.* I was heavy. I was a bag of bricks, I was drowning in my misery. I was shutting them out, not letting them in. I was worrying the people around me. Them not understanding, not knowing what to do, how to respond. Kyle was there in the distance. I sensed him, but I couldn't reach him, couldn't find him. I didn't want to, didn't want him to see me this way. I made myself invisible, but I guess I never was. I guess he was there the whole time, waiting for me. It was dark, everything felt so dark. I remember slipping like this. I remember before, feeling this way, going through this. I remember, but this was worse. This was impossible. This was *no clue how I was passing my classes, how I was even getting paid for my job.* It was so blurry. Hard to find the memories. Hard to go there. It was all black and I'm sure I was impossible, I remember, trying to breathe, trying to move, trying to interact, and every moment crashing me back down.

> *Lily is curled up on her bed in a dark room. It looks like daylight outside but dark drapes are pulled over the windows. The hum of a ceiling fan is the only sound in the room until a knock on the door breaks the silence. Lily is quiet, she stares at the door but remains paralyzed in the bed.*
>
> *"Lily," a girl's voice says sweetly from behind the door.*
>
> *The jingling of the door knob follows. Lily is still, in a daze, a trance, not there, somewhere else. There is more fidgeting with the door and suddenly it opens and a girl comes through the door, Kyle is with her.*
>
> *"Lily are you ok?" the girl says as she slowly enters the room.*
>
> *"Get the hell out of my room," Lily jumps up.*
>
> *"Lily, we want to help you, what can we do?"*
>
> *Kyle stands at the entrance to the room, observing, not speaking, taking it all in. Watching the love of his life enraged, on edge, falling apart. He is strong, sturdy. A rock.*

I don't know how we got through it. I don't know how he stayed there, watched me. I didn't even have the energy to fight it. And it was months passing. It was drawn out. And when I came out on the other end, so many people were gone. I was alone. I had pushed them all away. My depression, my insanity, turned to rage. The words I hated saying, didn't want to say, didn't mean to say. But they came out. They came out, I exposed them, and they were gone, I couldn't pull them back in. But I couldn't change it, or take it back. I wanted to scream, my words were coming, they were vindictive, and they were uncalled for. What was I trying to prove? Maybe it was a test. Maybe it was me trying to see who would really be there, who I could count on. But that would have been worse. I wasn't even capable of those thoughts. I couldn't even get there in my mind, it was just a cloud. A big black cloud and I was shrinking under it.

## Chapter 50

## *and we keep saying goodbye.*

I should have said something at the beginning. I should have stopped it from going further with Kyle, but I lacked the control to take myself down. I lacked the control to act on my anger toward myself. I was missing something. I was lost. I needed a friend, someone to go to, talk to, confess. I was guilty. I needed a way out. But every time I inched closer to something, anytime I allowed someone in, let them get close, my body shut down, my mind shut off. I was paralyzed emotionally. This was not going to work out. This would not be ok. I had to learn that. I had to accept that.

I was unable to explain myself. I was trying to work through it. I was sensitive. I was needing love. I was needing attention. I set the bar way too high and there were no mistakes allowed. And the thing was, I was making all the mistakes. I was rewriting the laws. I was changing history. But I held my ground. Growing up I took these baby steps, thinking too deeply about slumber parties and overnights, over analyzing. Before saying too much. Never trusting. Never depending on anyone. Always assuming the worst. Always assuming nothing was safe, nothing sacred. I didn't understand where these fears, these restrictions came from. Was it the stuff sitting inside of me, drowning me? Was it the fear of being found out? Was it the privacy instilled deep in my being from childhood. How much was the disease. How much was me, it was all me and I was all diseased. I was wanting to see things clearly and assuming the impossible. It was impossible.

I was the *short term friend* girl. I was the *best friends forever, change my mind the next day* kind of girl. I was the girl who gave too much. The girl embarrassed by her honesty. Her vulnerability. I was the girl who dated the guys, and moved on. The girl who made friends and moved on. There wasn't much difference between my relationships with guys and my friends then. And maybe that never changed. So many years defined by these friendships. These afraid to give too much. It was twisted. It was *how much can I give of myself.* How much can I share of myself. And I did what I could. And time got in the middle and changed things. Time destroyed me. And it was all just another excuse why I couldn't commit. To a friend. A guy. Anything. I was mind changing all the time. I was *this is my destiny, loneliness.*

And looking back there were the big memories. The people who were there for the major moments. The people who made an impact. But I was running out so fast. I was losing it before it even began. Those moments, and those memories, always easier to run from than face. And it was simple then. Simple to just walk away. And the older you get, the older I got, the more I knew. The less I felt. The more numb I was. The easier it was to walk away without a sound. The easier it was to write it off, to write them off. To not care. To not feel. What was hard at first. What I felt in the pit of my stomach, what I knew I should feel. Knew I should feel guilt for. Those things, they were so dim. So faint. They were questions without answers, they were who I was and who I wasn't at the same time. I wanted to change something. I wanted to learn. Wanted to fall. Wanted to fail. But I was always failing. Always not good enough. Always comparing myself. Always hoping for more, for something different. And I needed a second chance. I needed a million chances.

In the early years it was girl scouts. It was track meets. It was the friends I made in these places. It was me sort of going through the motions. Me being a kid. But then too, I set the bar too high. Got hurt. The twisting and turning even then. I remember this girl. This best friend. Our parents were friends, so we by association were friends. But it kept growing, and we were inseparable. And I remember it being good, so good to have a friend. We lived in different areas, so we spent most of the weekends together. Slumber parties. Girl stuff. Everything was great, until one day it changed. One day my mind slipped into the not good enough. It slipped into some strange jealousy. Me feeling alone. Lost. I don't really remember the exact event, maybe it was a series of things that got it there. But I just remember the anger. The rage. The how could you. The grudge. One Sunday at my house. She came over with her dad and I told her I hated her. Never wanted to see her again. I try and think back, try to get in touch with what hurt me. What made me run from it. And I can't find it. I threw those memories away, and let go of them, released them. Tore them in pieces so they couldn't hurt me anymore. Memories are strange like that. Some of the bad ones, they always seem to haunt you, and others, they vanish, so far away you can't get them back.

As I got older, as I started making my own friends. Choosing who I'd hang out with. Who my best friend would be, I went through a million phases. The friends you had because you didn't want to be alone. The friends you had because there was nothing better to do. The friends you had because you were in the same classes and you needed someone to keep you company. There were the inseparable relationships, that lasted a year. Then you changed, they changed. You grew apart. You got tired. I was always getting tired. The start of middle school was interesting. It was the clash between my friends and them, wanting to be popular, wanting more. Me not good enough. Or maybe me just not caring enough. It was a popularity contest and I didn't want to play. And the close friends became acquaintances. And as time passed as we all got older, those friends remained at a distance, but we always had those times. Those moments. Those young girls figuring out life moments.

There were the friends who judged me. Made fun of me. The not really friends, friends. There was me thinking I could fit in, not realizing who I was. What it all meant. There were these girls so annoying. Complaining about these tiny things, when my head was about to explode. When my heart was beating outside of my chest. It was impossible to understand, but I thought I was supposed to. So I tried. And I failed. And I walked away. All of these years, one by one. Me spending every moment with this person, that person. Me moving on. Walking away. Too vulnerable. Too many secrets shared. And I didn't want to let go. I didn't want to show all of my cards. No trust. I was always paranoid. Always thinking what I had would be lost. Some petty fight. There were the best friends I lost to the new girls who moved to town. And soon I wasn't enough. And it only reinforced what I already knew.

And when I got to high school, I was so often the girl with the boyfriend. And I wasn't sure I wanted to be that girl. I didn't want that. Didn't want to rely on that. So I made my friends. But it was still the same thing. The get close, then walk away. The pour myself into one world only to get bored. Need out. There were the few friends that lasted through everything. We changed together. Grew together. We shifted in and out of different groups, different obligations, different things, but we would always go back to each other. There were a couple of those. And those were good. But those ones, they were hard. Sometimes impossible. And I was pouring down my madness on the ones who were closest to me. I was fine one day and a wreck the next. I was all over the place. I was trying to keep calm. Trying to keep it simple. Trying to blend into the background. I was good at this or that, but I was never good enough. There were the close knit groups. And within those groups there were the phases of friends. The best friends one month, barely talked the next and it would rotate around. On and on until it never made sense. But they came at a time when things were at their worse, and those ones, they were there for the big moments. The moments that were tiny. The things I allowed them to see, and those I kept inside. Those things that came out on their own without me knowing. And they allowed me to be there, for someone else. Me trying to put my energy into another person instead of being consumed by the beast. This monster, it got in the way of everything. Me never wanting to get too close. Always keeping my distance. And as time passed, as I moved on, as I grew, and I avoided, so much changed, and so much stayed the same.

The college years. My insecurities bubbling to the surface. Me sinking into deep bouts of depression. The bad months, the ones that tore me away from everything that meant anything to me. And there were those bad days, when everything I built, all these relationships, these friendships I worked at, I tore them down. I pushed everyone away. I tested my limits. I played the game, played my hand, all in. And I lost it all. In a few months I lost it all. When the storm had quieted, I slowly tried to get it back. To regain so much that I lost of my friendships. I couldn't remember the bad. I couldn't remember those moments where I was an animal, like a drunk's blackouts. I had these emotional blackouts. Me responsible for so much. Me testing the limits. Me not stopping. Saying too much. Hurting. I could feel the blood on my fingertips, and I ripped them up. And I remember the sting of the words as they came out of my mouth. I remember wanting to pull them back, take it all back in. I remember all of those things, but the big things. The words, the actual moments, those things I can't get back. I can't find them. I remember dark rooms. I remember shutting down. I remember thinking I should stop, and I remember being unable to move. I remember the faces when I finally came out of it, when I could breathe again. I remember the eyes, stained with hurt. And I remember wishing I could remember exactly, specifically what is was. But I couldn't get myself back there. Those memories so faded. My mind not allowing me to get there. So many times like that. So many memories of relationships that have become clouded by the monster. I couldn't even feel the pain but I knew I should have. I knew I should have been destroyed by it, but instead I used it to destroy.

## Chapter 51

## it's never simple.

I don't really know how I came out on the other end. I had never been in so deep before. So much time I had spent, running, hiding, feeding the monster bit by bit. I felt it grow inside of me, then I would starve it, push it back down. Giving it life and taking it away. It was destroying me, and I finally saw that. I finally realized what this thing was doing to me. Where it was taking me. I didn't want to go there anymore. Finally, me realizing I needed something to change. Couldn't do it alone. I had to take care of myself, had to figure it out. So often I was told that people with this disorder, they won't take their pills, can't take them, have the hardest time with it. And I was barely taking mine. Hated the idea of taking something for the rest of my life. Hated the idea of being chained down to this. I fought it so hard.

And at the end of it, when I finally felt some sunlight on my skin, he was there, Kyle was sitting there waiting. He was brown eyes, he was strong, he was soft, and he was perfect. He had to be half as crazy as me to stay, to be there, to walk through this with me. I didn't understand. Could not figure out how someone could give that much of themselves. How they could be beaten down, stand back up, and hold on. I tried to warn him. Told him I could be there again, in that place, maybe worse. That it was unpredictable. That it was impossible to tell. But he still stood there, him, he was un-shifting. And I knew then I had to figure something out. Work something out. I needed to get better, as good as I could be. Whatever it meant I needed to do it. Because this guy, I wasn't ready to lose him.

When I followed up with my doctor I finally confessed I wasn't consistent with my medications. I was having a hard time with them. She put me on something different, something new, a one pill fix that was supposed to be a lot easier, less major side effects. And I really wanted to change. I really wanted to get better, as good as I could get. It was a slow process. It was okay days. It was me hating myself, wondering what I did wrong. What I did to deserve this. Deserve. I hated that word but I was a slave to it. I was screaming, hating myself, hating my mind, and my body. Everything. Everything sort of faded into the background. I was trying to rebuild what I had lost. Trying to prove to myself I could care enough about someone to try. Try when I had no desire to do anything. Try when all I wanted to do was go to bed and never wake up. Because the thing was, even with better meds, even being consistent, it just made it all a little more stable. It helped the highs to be smaller and the lows to be shorter, not as deep, not as consuming. But it didn't fix it, didn't make it better, it just eased it a little. I had to work for it. I had to fight for it. And most of the time I didn't want to, and it would have been easier not to. It would have been back to the same routine. Never get too close, run before it gets too deep. And I could live that way, if I really wanted, but it was hard to walk away. The idea of leaving Kyle, of just getting out of there, I thought about it, toyed with it. But then I would see him, be near him. It was butterflies, it was electric. It was, *I never want to lose this feeling*, good. And so I had to stay. Had to try, had to give all I could, before giving up. I was fighting the demons. I sort of knew it was impossible to beat them, to get rid of them, make them disappear. But I could work on the other stuff. The rage. The outbursts. The impulses. I could bite my tongue. I could figure out the past. The stuff that built up while I was slowly dying inside. The things I let get to me, I let destroy me. My mom, pushing me down, never enough. My dad, present and absent at the same time. My baby sister, raging, and the guilt, not there, me never there enough. Samantha, her issues, problems. Their battles. Them putting me in a corner. Them blaming me. I was perfect. I was the perfect one. And I hid my secret. Kept it inside. Fought it alone, then, and now. I didn't trust, didn't feel. Couldn't be vulnerable. Didn't want to cry, didn't want to deal with the stuff, everything building up. So I confided in Kyle. I ran to him. And he let me. Let me be myself. Let me screw up, and pick up the pieces, and do it all over again. Me trying to deal with the consequences of my actions. Trying to deal with where I came from, what I had been. Before him. Before he found me, before he sat there, listened. Tried to understand. Tried to build me back up. Tried to open my eyes. See deeper than the surface. And I wanted to regret everything I had done. The things I wasn't proud of. I had covered up, suffocated my emotions. I had loved, I had thought I loved so many times. But I knew deep down that wasn't true. That I didn't know how to love. But the ones I chose, the ones I let in, wished I had let in. They were the stepping stones, I wanted to hate myself for everything, but at the same time I couldn't regret. Every moment. Every complicated thing I brought into this, everything I pushed down inside, the journey. All of that, it brought me here. Brought me to this man. This man who took me for who I was. No strings attached. No expectations. All he wanted was for me to hold on. Hold on long enough to love him. And for the first time, I wanted to love. I wanted to believe in love the way it was supposed to be. The way it should be. All the times, the times someone tried, tried to get in. Wanted to be let in. I put up the defenses, put up the walls. So afraid of this monster that was consuming every part of my being. This thing I didn't understand. Couldn't comprehend. It fought to break free. Fought to overpower me. So I shut down. I shut it off, I broke down. I tortured

215

myself. Allowed myself to be broken. To be bruised from the inside out, and I hated myself. What I had allowed myself to become. So afraid to show emotion, affection, so afraid to feel. And finally, finally I wanted to feel.

I wanted to stare into him. Wanted to know him. Explore him. Challenge him. I wanted to be for him what he was for me. I wanted it two sided. Everything had been uneven. Never enough of myself. But him, this man, he reached inside of me. Pulled me out. Exposed me to myself. And instead of running, I stayed. I talked about it. Threatened it. Screamed it. But I didn't want it. I never wanted it. I just wanted him. I wanted peace. I wanted silence. I wanted to sleep at night. I wanted to let go. Let him in, and keep him there. It was so easy, so easy to just walk away. To let him in for a moment, then walk away. Hurt him. Destroy him. I wanted to fight him. I wanted to argue, prove he was a fraud. Like I had been. The things I did. I wanted to just convince him that he didn't really love me. That he couldn't love me. That it could never work. I was vicious. I was up and down. I was medicated, more stable, but still scared. Terrified. Distant. Alone. Empty. I was nothing. He was brave. He was out on a limb, taking a chance on me. He truly believed from the beginning that he loved me, that he would always love me. I wanted to think it obsessive. To think he was insane. Insane like me. To think this could work. But I wanted it to. I wanted to believe it. Just like he had. I hesitated. I stepped backward and he moved closer. He wasn't going to let me off that easy. He wasn't going to give up on me.

## Chapter 52

## *falling.*

There was a moment in time, halfway through my college years, when I sunk. When I let down the walls. When I recognized the cage, when I admitted it. Confessed it to myself. I had been tortured. Tortured by myself. I was ready and terrified at the same time. There was Kyle. His perfection. His stability. As I elevated him in my mind. I was lost, exposed. A fraud. And I couldn't fight it anymore. I had loved him. Without question. I had loved him, without understanding. I had loved him for the person he let me be. Myself. This girl, this lost girl I never knew or understood. I had stunted her. Pushed her down. Fighting the urges. Allowing the impulses. Acting on the numbness. The pain. I had pushed her aside. I had let her get away, cage herself. Never letting anyone in, only a taste. Only a glimpse of myself. Just enough to be loved, but never enough to love back. Burning bridges. Not looking back. Not looking back because I knew then I was incapable of feeling that. Of feeling what I had done. But now I saw it. I felt it. I stared it straight in the mirror. Analyzing each point. Each moment in time. Finding meaning in the tiny things, the maybe insignificant things. I was *never able to make up for my past*, crazy. I was *losing the battle*, insane. But I was head over heels in love. I was lost in the sun. I was holding on to nothing. I was out on the edge. Looking down. Ready to fall. I was, *what was I thinking* crazy. I was, *time to let go*. I was ready. I was *back and forth.* I was *pros and cons.* And I was free. Free because I released myself.

This was good.

## Chapter 53

## something good for a change.

Those days, it wasn't always bad. There were these moments of clarity. The glimpses of sanity. There was the good, there were the accomplishments. There were the *how did I come so far, reach so much*. There was dazed. There was questioning everything. There were people saying I was strong. There was me, for a few moments, believing them. Because me, I was going through hell, had gone through hell. Not quite coming out on the other side but I was getting there. I was gaining stability. I was being honest with myself for the first time. Ever. Remembering being young. Remembering even then, hiding. Even then, afraid to feel. Afraid of my thoughts. Afraid of the lies that just came out, automatic. And now, now I was climbing back. I was on my knees surrendering. I was cursing, pleading. I was begging for the pain to go away. Because even with the meds. Even with the coming clean. Even with the honesty. The openness, even with that, there was still the pain. The knot in my stomach. The racing thoughts. The monster, consuming me. There was me, wanting to rip my stomach out, but I feared it would just come back. It would move throughout me. It was all over me already, and it was there. Always there, in the back of my mind. Mocking me. It never failed. No matter how good I was, how much I tried to change, tried to get better, it was still there lingering. It was supposed to let me go. I had released it. I had released myself. But it didn't leave. Stayed close. Looking over my shoulder. And me, I was trying to stand on my feet.

I was starting to see a little reward for the hard work. I was getting. Receiving. The validation some tiny part of me needed. The words I never really heard. Good job. I was searching for a voice. And I was finding it. I was finding an outlet, and I was finding people. Open doors.

I had my mind set on graduation. On finally ending the education part of my life. On loving the work I was doing. I was so ready to move forward. So ready to take the next step. The times when my mind wanted to shut down. Wanted to just quit. So close to the finish line. This finish line, and I just wanted to stop. Wanted to throw in the towel. Stay in bed. Walk away. But I fought for it. Despite the downs, the can't sleeps. The can't turn it off's. I just pushed. Kept moving. Head down. Eyes closed so tight. And I fought. Against myself. Tooth and nail. I was a bloody mess, kicking myself to get up. To keep going. To try again. And when I would mess up. When I would forget. Make a mistake. All those voices came back, chased me back down the road. The never good enough. The screw up. The you will never be anything. Can't do anything road. But it wasn't as bad as it could have been. And when the days were okay. When nothing terrible happened, it was a good day. And it felt like I was having more of those. More nothing terrible. Nothing that brought me down, collapsed me, then it was okay. And then it was one day at a time. It was just this. If I can just get through this. And that's how I did it, that's how I made it through those last few months. Last few weeks. That's how I survived myself.

## Chapter 54

## new beginnings.

My graduation present was an engagement ring. It was unexpected, but much desired. It caught me off guard. Still on this cloud of how could he love me. Still thinking, is he sure he can do this? Be with me. It was this scary feeling, trusting someone enough to build a life with them. Me always wanting to run away. Always knowing when it came down to it I could get into the car and drive. No turning back. But the ring, this thing circling my finger, that was a little more permanent. It was the end of the run, the end of the walking away. Walking out. Leaving it all unfinished. Leaving the I love you's. Me always burning bridges. Give so much, just enough to get close. Just enough for them to be vulnerable, for them to trust me, and then I was gone. With relationships, with friendships, anything. There were no survivors when I was done. But this, this had to be different. I said yes, and I meant it, but the second Kyle put that ring on my finger my mind was off. Off and running. Spinning. Thinking over and over all the possibilities, the what if's. So disconnected. Happy and obsessed at the same time. Obsessed with figuring out every last detail. Every unexpected moment. I was driving myself mad, and he watched me. He let me. He let me spin myself in circles, and when I grew tired, he let me fall asleep in his arms.

The two of us together the idea was so crazy. Me insane. Always on edge. Always thinking. Always screaming inside. And him off the walls, crazy enough to love me. I couldn't imagine another person with the ability to be with me. To understand me. To accept me. Someone I was willing to do the same for. And I thought back to all those years ago, walking across the grass on my college campus and him, getting under my skin. And we both knew then, knew without really knowing, that we would end up here one day. Him driving me crazy. Him there when I wanted to be alone. Always there, always present. And me, always expecting him to leave. And he didn't. He proved me wrong. No matter how much I tested him. Tried to convince him he couldn't do this forever. Couldn't stay. He proved me wrong. He challenged me. Didn't let me get away with it. Didn't let me give up on myself. He wanted more for me. And I wanted everything for him.

# Chapter 55

## *shattered.*

And for a while things were okay. We were all in wedding plans. I was still closed down. Still *don't get too close.* But I was learning. I was slowly changing. On the good days, my chest was still empty, and I would feel these aches in the pit of my stomach. The monster letting out a roar. Letting me know it was still there, still present. I was on guard. I was *don't get too comfortable, the quiet before the storm.* I was *good days and bad days.* But I was in love, and I was loved. I was functioning. I was breathing.

And one day, one of those off days. One of those wake up not right days, it snuck up on me. Me - going through the motions, slowly moving, this sinking feeling following me around, relentless. I felt aches in my body, a rumbling in the pit of my stomach. I wanted to scream, wanted to claw at my skin. I wanted the day to just end, and it was only getting started. And it was that day, that day I got a phone call that would change everything, complicate everything. The call telling me my little sister was dead. She had died. She was gone.

And the monster awoke from its quiet slumber. And a fire grew within me. And I was *on the floor, collapsing* crazy. I was *don't touch me my skin is on fire,* crazy. I was freezing. I was walking without moving. I was gone. My body vacant. Only the monster hadn't left, it devoured me completely. And I laid there, a crumbled mess. And I let it take me. I barely fought. Barely felt it as it consumed me. And then it was me, a zombie, a mess, walking but barely moving, talking and barely saying a thing. It was months of no work, sleeping, never leave the house. Stay in bed. A safe routine. It was late nights. Can't sleep, can't ever sleep. Reruns. Infomercials. It was empty. It was dark. It was everything we had built falling down. It was Kyle trying to hold me together, and me pulling myself apart.

Everything was a blur for the most part. For a while the memories are faint, I can barely touch them. Feel them. It was a funeral, it was weeks back home, it was *how the hell did I get there, how did I get back*. Some nightmare world. Some detachment. Some second guessing. Me remembering all the things I did wrong. Everything I could have changed. Me being so far away for so long. Wishing I could go back. Wishing I could get those few moments back and replay them over again. Relive them. The do over moments and the never change them moments. And I was gone. I was all monster. I was *leave me alone don't talk to me*. Touch me. Look at me. I was scared of my own shadow. And Kyle was there beside me. Filling in the blanks. The gaps. Always there. Never changing. And I was *black heart*. I was *wish I were dead*. And those days. Weeks. Months. They were impossible. Never were, never ending they were a disaster. Me and him, fighting to stay above water. And I was at peace knowing I had him to help me through this, but at the same time I never wanted to get through it. I didn't want to survive it. I was numb inside. I was ripping my insides out to see if there was anything there. I was *wish it was me instead of her*. I was playing god. I was a mess. But I was clinging on. I was white knuckles. I was skin cracking. Bleeding inside.

My body was slowly shutting down. I was *stomach pains*. I was *skin*. I was *doctors*. Emergency rooms. Office visits. I was *medications*. I was *a thin thread about to rip*. And Kyle he was quiet eyes. He was soft, and he was a rock. He was *lean on me* there, and I was *breaking inside*. I was broken. I was, *I will never survive this*. I was questioning. I was looking for answers. I was not wanting to know the truth. But it was inside of me. And it was overtaking me. This wasn't the plan. This wasn't the way things were supposed to be. Me finally learning to survive myself. Now me, ready to die. Wanting it more than ever. Every pain I ever felt. The monster, magnified. Empty. Consumed, and paralyzed. This was my life. And me, I was a shadow of myself.

*the end.*

# Epilogue

## Surviving.

They say time heals all, but it doesn't.

I thought I deserved a happily ever after. I thought maybe I was even on my way. I hate that word, deserved. I wish I could find every dictionary in the world and scribble over its existence. In the lowest pits, the depths of the grave, the struggle with the monster, the battle with myself, I thought about fairness. About life, about death. About being missed, about being forgotten. I thought about death a lot more than life. I thought about relationships. About memories. About failure and regrets. I wondered where I was and where I was going and how I would ever get there. I thought about happiness, if I even knew what that was. I imagined it was unattainable. I thought about a wedding, about a union, about commitment. I thought about living life after loss. And I thought about being with someone forever despite the monster fighting me at every turn. I thought I was making all the wrong decisions. I thought about going home, about running away from this new life and finding a sense of safety in my past. I thought about those long lost loves, the unreachable things, the friendships faded - I thought I needed those instead. Anything but where I was, where I am. I thought nothing lasts, everything so faded, fading, vanishing - so why does it matter? And I thought if that's true then was the monster forever, was the pain forever, was loneliness, and sadness, and destruction forever? I didn't find all the answers, but I asked myself a lot of questions. And I'm still asking. Because for every thought about leaving, about running, hiding, or ending it all, I keep finding another side, another story, another question. It isn't much, but right now, this is me.

Surviving. . .

# Acknowledgments:

To Alex - for inspiring me.
To my husband for his unfailing love – for helping me get the courage to find my voice, my family for their unending support and being imperfectly perfect, and my friends for their truth and guidance.
Mom & Dad thank you for always believing.
Jerzy thank you for your wisdom and for being my partner-in-crime on some of my greatest adventures.
Birdy thank you for your courage.
LK thank you for a lifetime of memories, forever.
RJH thank you for understanding my heart.
Turtle thank you for always taking my side.
Grams thanks for always checking on me and the status of this book, I hope it was worth the wait.
Anthony thank you for your beautiful photography.
To everyone throughout the years who encouraged me and spurred me on toward this moment, I could not have done this without you.
Special thanks to Nicole and Julie for your notes, feedback, direction, and constant support.
And of course to Coppola for lying patiently at my feet as I worked.

Made in the USA
Charleston, SC
01 December 2011